MASTERPIECES OF
HORROR

Compiled by Rosamund Morris

HART PUBLISHING COMPANY, INC.
New York City, New York

ACKNOWLEDGMENTS

Grateful acknowledgment is made to the copyright owners for permission to reprint the following stories:

"The Price of the Head" by John Russell; copyright 1916 by P. F. Collier & Son, reprinted by kind permission of Brandt & Brandt.

"Granny's Birthday" from *Nightmares and Geezenstacks* by Fredric Brown; copyright 1961 by Fredric Brown, reprinted by kind permission of Bantam Books, Inc.

"Terror" by Will F. Jenkins; copyright 1946 by Will F. Jenkins, reprinted by kind permission of the author.

"The Adventure of the Engineer's Thumb" from *The Adventures of Sherlock Holmes* by Sir Arthur Conan Doyle; reprinted by kind permission of the Trustees of the Estate of Sir Arthur Conan Doyle and John Murray, Ltd.

"Two Bottles of Relish" by Lord Dunsany, reprinted from *Story Magazine;* copyright 1936 by Story Magazine, Inc., reprinted by kind permission of Story Magazine.

"The Monkey's Paw" by W. W. Jacobs; reprinted by kind permission of The Society of Authors as the literary representatives of the Estate of W. W. Jacobs.

"The Speckled Band" from *The Adventures of Sherlock Holmes* by Sir Arthur Conan Doyle; reprinted by kind permission of the Trustees of the Estate of Sir Arthur Conan Doyle and John Murray, Ltd.

"Trapped!" by H. Vernor Dixon, originally published in *This Week* magazine; copyright 1950 by H. Vernor Dixon, reprinted by kind permission of Harold Ober Associates Inc.

"Wine on the Desert," by Max Brand, copyright, 1936, by Frederick Faust; reprinted by kind permission of Brandt & Brandt.

CONTENTS

WILL F. JENKINS *(1898-   )*

. . . lives in Virginia, where he was born. Under the name of Murray Leinster, he published his first story in 1915 at the age of 17. In 1932, Jenkins discarded his pseudonym, and has been writing under his own name ever since. His stories have been translated into 16 languages and are available on every continent.

From his years of writing pulp fiction, Jenkins evolved a plain, clear style, coherent plot lines, and, most typically, swift pacing. Though "Terror" runs to more than 25 pages, it seems considerably shorter because each episode in the story moves quickly and directly to the next.

Alone with a homicidal maniac,

Jane faces pure

TERROR

JANE WAVED a cordial good-by as the car turned about before the yet unopened cottage. She continued to wave as it rumbled off into the woods-road with a farewell blast of its horn. It droned away toward the main highway, and Jane felt a curious loneliness as it vanished among the trees all about.

That was absurd, of course. A camp-out week end at the family cottage by the lake was nothing to be lonely about. Her guests would be arriving in a couple of hours, and George Holloway had said he'd be out extra early to help get the place opened up. She ought to unlock the door and raise the windows and start to get ready. But she stood still, listening to the noise of the car as it grew fainter and fainter with distance.

She was definitely early. There might be somebody coming out to one of the other cottages about the small lake's shores, but there would be no one else here yet. At the moment, indeed, there was probably no other human being within miles, save the friends who'd brought her up and dropped her off on the way to their own cottage farther out of town. And the sound of their car grew fainter and fainter.

Standing solitary in the sunshine, Jane suddenly shivered. She felt that eerie, hair-raising tingle of the nerves all along in her spine which, when they experience it, makes people say, "A rabbit jumped over my grave." But there was no reason for it. The air was warm and still. Lifelessly drooping weeds near the gateway reflected the sun's heat. All the world was completely tranquil. . . . But the tingling came again. It was like a chill of pure, causeless terror in all the shining brightness of midday.

Then she realized that she couldn't hear the car any longer. Irrelevantly, it occurred to her that those in the car couldn't hear her, either, even if she screamed. Then she heard a rustling in the underbrush on the far side of the woods-road. She caught her breath sharply.

The rustling ceased. Insects shrilled senselessly. Small wavelets on the lake lapped against the beached rowboat, tied to its stake. There were all the innumerable sounds of absolute solitude, but not a single sound expressive of humanity, not even a dog barking or a rooster crowing. There was nobody around. Nobody. Jane felt a completely irrational contraction of her throat. Of course, that rustling in the bushes must have been caused by a squirrel or a chipmunk.

She resolutely picked up her bag and walked to the door of the cottage. She put in her key and unlocked it. The sound of its opening echoed cavernously from within. The inside smelled close and faintly musty. She went in. She closed the door firmly behind her. Somehow, it was comforting to have a locked door between her and the solitude without.

She went back to the kitchen, glanced in, and saw a bowl of withered wild flowers no one had remembered to empty out the week end before. She climbed upstairs to change before beginning the opening ceremonies. But the mustiness did make her open the windows of the front bedroom. The fresh air was comforting. She changed briskly and so far recovered from her unreasonable unease that she found herself thinking of George Holloway, who should arrive almost any minute now to help open up the cottage. She felt a mild and slightly wicked curiosity about his reason for coming out especially early to be so helpful.

Really, he was going to explain something nobody else would have bothered about. Last night she'd taken the family maid home, driving her because a heavy rain was falling and the girl had worked long after the usual time. She'd seen George on her way back, just as she stopped at the traffic light nearest her maid's home. George had nearly walked into her car in the rain. He had a girl with him, and both were getting soaked, and he was arguing savagely with her, and the girl was crying. Her crying seemed to make George angrier.

Jane had rolled down a window and cheerily offered them a lift. George had stared at her—glared, rather—and curtly refused, saying they hadn't far to go. She'd had one glimpse of the girl's woebegone face, with wet, blonde curls around it. And then the traffic light changed and she drove on.

She'd been mildly curious. Where the maid lived was not exactly the best part of town. And George Holloway—in his late thirties and meticulous and restrained and impeccable—definitely did not belong there. He'd writhe at having been seen in such surroundings.

He had. Now, tying the straps of her halter-top at the back of her neck, she was amused at the memory of his phone call. It came an hour after she got home, at eleven-thirty. He was profusely apologetic and explained anxiously that he'd met this girl to try to settle and hush up a scandal that she'd gotten someone they both knew involved in. He hoped Jane hadn't mentioned seeing him. . . . She hadn't. . . . He was relieved. He said he'd come out to the cottage extra early and help her open up, and tell her the story. He knew he could trust to her discretion, and it meant keeping one of the finest marriages he knew from going on the rocks.

Up in the slant-ceilinged bedroom, Jane picked up the garments she'd changed from and moved to hang them up in the small, cramped closet. She looked forward zestfully to giving George a bad half-hour, pretending that she thought he was trying to cover up a romance of his own. She opened the closet door.

And her heart stopped. She caught her breath.

Someone had been in it. She didn't keep much in the closet, but everything had been shifted about and clumsily put back. As she stared, dazedly, a misplaced fold of cloth dropped back into place. It gave the feeling that the closet had been ransacked merely minutes or only seconds since.

Jane's throat clicked to tightness. Her heart hammered against her ribs. She had never been the fainting sort, but she felt herself go ashy-white, and she suddenly found herself listening desperately. She listened for the creaking of a loose board somewhere or the shuffling sound of a footstep on a stair. And she was agonizedly conscious that there was no one to hear if she screamed for help.

Somebody had been in the cottage. Somebody had ransacked this room—and carefully tried to replace everything—but everybody knew the lakeside cottages were usually occupied on week ends. So any sneak thief who knew he had time to replace what he touched must have broken in during the week. Days ago.

Jane told herself that. She repeated it. She assured herself that she believed it. But it was on trembling legs and with wide, scared eyes that she essayed to go downstairs again. She could get a carving knife from the kitchen, anyhow—

It was miles down the steps to the ground floor, and the journey took centuries. It seemed to her that her whole body shook with the violent beating of her heart. Yet nothing had happened. Nothing at all. She turned into the kitchen with her knees about to give way under her, and the cutlery rattled as she fumbled for something to serve as a weapon.

But George would be here presently. She had the door locked. She would be all right until he came. She was just scared. It must have happened days ago. She repeated her self-assurances like a litany and tried desperately to believe them. But she was breathing very quickly. She looked about the kitchen almost like a hunted animal. A narrow streak of sunlight lay across the floor. The shutters of one of the windows were not tightly fastened. In the narrow line of sunshine there lay a petal from one of the withered flowers which drooped in the bowl that had not been emptied last week. Her eyes flicked to the speck of color and went on, and then returned. Then they clung in utter, fascinated horror.

The floor was wet. Her eyes moved in stunned jerkings to the table. To the bowl of water with the withered flowers. It stood by the window. It had been spilled and refilled. Recently. Somebody had been in the cottage today. Within an hour. Within minutes! Someone had come in the kitchen window. A glance made her heart race in terror. The window was not fastened down. Someone had come in it and spilled the flowers and ransacked the closet upstairs and probably others, and then had come back and wiped up the floor and refilled the bowl. So their entry would not be suspected. So—so—

Jane's tongue clove to the roof of her mouth. Her hands shook uncontrollably, but a hysterical cunning warned her not to give any sign that she was suspicious

of alarm. Someone had been here only a little while ago.
He was probably still near. If she screamed—

There was no sound anywhere but the idiotic noise of
insects outside the house singing senselessly in the sunlight. No sound at all. No small creakings of flooring to
tell of movement within the house.

Shaking and trembling there in the shadowy kitchen
with its streak of sunlight on the floor, Jane found herself reasoning with a panicky, desperate logic. Whoever
had entered the cottage had guessed that somebody
would be coming today. But they couldn't have known
she'd come alone. If they had the intention to harm her,
still they wouldn't have dared wait inside the house.
They would wait outside to see if a planned crime was
possible. Now that they knew she was alone, still they'd
wait for her to come out. But they wouldn't know she
was warned. If she could only delay until George got
here—and he would come soon; he'd said he'd come
early—if she could only delay—

Her arms and legs were incredibly heavy and stiff. It
was unbelievable that she should be able to cross the
kitchen floor. It was impossible that she could turn the
window catch to lock the window down. But she did.
She didn't dare raise the sash to fasten the shutters securely, but they might be caught. In any case, nobody
could come back in the window without breaking the
glass.

That was a pitiful attempt to be calm, with panic
yammering at her temples. She wasn't sure that she was
alone in the house, and she had to make sure. Her teeth

chattered, and she prayed desperately that George Holloway would come soon. He wasn't the closest of her friends, by any means. He was too much older, and too reasoned and too rational and too much controlled ever to rouse any real warmth of feeling in her. But he was broad-shouldered and strong, and she would have clung to him in sobbing gratitude had she heard his voice.

In a precarious and brittle composure, her hands shaking and her fingers stiff and without strength, she added an ice pick to her armory. A carving knife in one hand and an ice pick in the other. But if she did encounter an intruder, she felt that she would be simply paralyzed with fright.

She slipped out of her sandals for silent movement. She left the kitchen, her breath coming in gasps. There were four rooms on the ground floor. She moved on tiptoe to search them, swallowing convulsively. Sometimes she panted for breath. Her chest hurt. Always she listened. Once—that was in the downstairs bedroom—she heard a sound behind her, and her heart stopped dead. But it was a book on the arm of a chair. She'd bumped the chair and the book had fallen. It was minutes before she could breathe again. The worst of all was looking into the closets. That took the desperation of a cornered rat. She had it. She looked into every one. At least two of them had been disturbed.

She was upstairs and had just finished the last closet in the back room when there was an assured, firm footstep on the porch outside. Then an authoritative knock sounded on the door.

Jane felt herself go limp and weak and almost hysterical with relief. That was George. George Holloway. A large lump came into her throat, so that she could not even sob happily at the release. She couldn't even call to answer the knock. She fairly tottered into the front bedroom and to the windows she'd opened there. Tears of gratitude made the world swim before her eyes. She put her head out, still pale but overwhelmed with the banishment of terror. George was here.

But it wasn't George. It was an unknown burly figure in soiled work clothes. Bushy and improbable whiskers flowed over the collar of his shirt. And he stood in a tense, crouched, listening attitude, straining his ears for sounds of movement within the house.

Then he tried the doorknob. Gently. Softly. Soundlessly.

The door was locked. Jane knew it, but the muscles of her heart seemed to ache with the strain of suspense. The man slowly and cautiously released the knob. He crouched and put his shoulder to the door. His feet braced. He strained against it, to push it in. The doorframe creaked, and Jane's nightmarish horror bubbled over in a sound which should have been a cry, but was actually no more than a hoarse croaking noise.

The man jerked his head upward. He stood upright and his mouth opened. He made implausible speechsounds: "Hnelephome messij fyou, ma'm."

Jane wanted to cry out again. This burly creature spoke in the unintelligible fashion of a man with a cleft palate. It was unspeakably horrible. He had ransacked the house secretly. He tried to open the door without sound. Now he gobbled at her that there was a telephone message for her. All the world became unreal. This could not be true! She was dreaming! She would wake.

"I'm not interested in telephone messages," she said, her voice wobbling. "Please go away."

He did not go. He continued to stare. Bushy, luxuriant whiskers covered a great part of his face. She gazed at him in hypnotic, horrified fascination. The whiskers were false. It was childish. It was horrible. It was insane! Insane! That was an explanation which offered no hope, but she forced her stiff features into a smile.

"For g-goodness sake!" she said brightly, through chattering teeth. "You frightened me! But see now! It's a joke! You're wearing false whiskers! You really scared me."

The figure merely gazed upward.

Jane went on desperately, her lips twisted into a smile, "I'll bet I know you! You're quite a joker, aren't you? But it isn't nice to frighten people. Really! Now, take off the whiskers and tell me what you really want. You don't want to be acting queerly when my friends come. They'll be here any instant, now."

She turned her eyes to the end of the woods-road, praying passionately that George would come. The man below her did not follow her gaze, but she knew he was listening.

"I hear my friends' car now," said Jane brightly. "You take off those false whiskers and tell me who you are and what you want. Tell me why you're here."

The man stirred. He walked heavily to the corner of the house. He turned the corner. He vanished.

Jane wanted to faint, but she could not. Instead, she flew to the back windows of the second floor. They were down and the shutters were closed, but she peered out, her heart battering at her ribs with what seemed like hammer-blows.

She saw the man. He went purposefully to the little shed in which were kept the oars for the rowboat and a supply of firewood for the living-room fireplace. He went into the shed. He came out again. He carried an ax. The ax. He came inexorably toward the house. He went out of sight, and she heard him fumbling with the shutters of the kitchen window. Then there was the crash of broken glass.

Jane made a little whimpering noise. She had the nightmarish sensation of paralysis, of being unable to move, of having her lungs refuse to work; she suffocated while she waited in utter impotence for doom to come to her.

Her mind seemed to scream, to cry out insanely to George Holloway, imploring him hysterically to hurry, hurry, hurry. He was coming early. He should get here soon. But she needed him now! She heard her own voice making inarticulate noises of pure animal panic. Her muscles were stiff and frozen. Then she heard a crash downstairs. The bowl of wilted flowers had been knocked to the floor for the second time as the man came in the window. She heard his footsteps in the kitchen. Her body still refused to stir. She had all the sensations of strangling paralysis that come in nightmares. Her thoughts fairly gibbered. She heard him move toward the stairs. He started up.

Then she screamed. As it echoed, she heard him begin to run up the stairs.

Then the paralysis broke, but it was not the everyday Jane who fled, panting and screaming shrilly, to the front bedroom. It was an automaton which continued to scream senselessly as it flung a bare leg over the sill of an open window, and gripped the sill with fingers possessing the strength of panic, and lowered itself from the window and let go, to drop a bare five feet and tumble to the earth, and leap up again with unbelievable speed and flee.

She heard a great crash. Her screaming had told him of her movements. He had flung down the stairs and out of the front door. He was after her. She heard his footsteps.

Then she could scream no longer. She ran, with the ghastly feeling of no progress which also is typical of nightmares. She saw herself about to run headlong into brushwood, and in purest horror realized that instead of fleeing towards the woods-road along which George would be coming, she had run away from it. In underbrush the man would catch her. She flung an anguished glance over her shoulder even as she dodged frantically to one side. He was no more than twenty yards behind her. He carried the ax. He ran clumsily but with a maniacal fixity of purpose.

He gained on her when she changed course. She found herself fleeing crazily toward the lake. He raced after her, the ax held at mid-handle, in readiness for use. She could not dodge again. The lakeshore was before her. He was gaining. He was only paces behind her. Panting, she fled into the water, and as it deepened she leaped forward in a long dive, swimming as she had never swum before.

She came to the surface, gasping, and turned fear-glazed eyes behind her. She heard no splashing of pursuit. He had stopped at the water's edge. He stood there, still staring at her intently.

He turned toward the shed from which he had brought the ax. Twice he turned and stared again. He went into the shed. He came out, carrying the oars for the rowboat. And the ax. He went toward the boat.

Jane swam frantically, but the lake was wide and the boat would row faster than she could possibly swim. There was the top of a pine sapling sticking out of the water halfway across the lake. It had been forced into the bottom mud to serve as a marker for a swimming race early in the season. It told her that she could not possibly reach the other shore in time.

There was no hope at all, and with the realization came a peculiar numb clarity of thought. He would overtake her. He might kill her with the ax from the boat, or he might merely stun her with an oar and watch her drown in the lake's cool water. Then he would probably go away, and when George Holloway came he would find the house open and Jane vanished, and there would be no sign anywhere of what had happened save a broken windowpane and a spilled bowl of withered flowers.

She heard the sound of the man's feet on the bottom-boards of the rowboat. The sound came with uncanny distinctness through the water. She could not reach the opposite shore before he overtook her. She could not turn about and reach land before he could head her off. With the dazed horror of the doomed, she knew it. But when she heard the squeaking of oars in the row-locks—he was coming after her—the noise galvanized her into such a frenzy of effort that she strangled and went under.

The sound of oars continued to come through the water. Rhythmic. Steady. Inexorable. Merciless. She began to lose her head, and something warned her, "If you lose your head you'll drown." But frenzy clawed at her reason. And there was a return of the hysterical cunning which had helped her before.

She went under, splashing foolishly. She came up again, not swimming, but merely thrashing about like someone in whom panic and exhaustion had destroyed all reason. Then she seemed to fight desperately to pull away from the boat, but with a vast amount of wasted strength. And then she went under again, and came up in a smother of foam and cried out throatily, and went under once more. This time it was final.

She opened her eyes underwater and saw the weird, sunlit submarine world. She saw the rippled surface above her, stretching into invisibility on every hand save where the bottom of the rowboat broke it. She saw the oar blade dip down to visibility and rise again. She swirled in the water and swam desperately for the vague shape which was the submerged part of the pine sapling which had been sunk in the mud for a race marker.

She came up behind it. She fought to breathe quietly, clamping her jaws lest her teeth chatter. She let herself sink, and saw the boat again. It paused and turned. The man was hunting for her. He had seen the splashings, which were, convincingly, cramps or pure panic. He searched and searched. She rose and breathed. She saw the boat come purposefully toward the sapling, whose top projected above water. She went under, and remained there until she thought her lungs would burst. The boat, overhead, circled the sapling while he peered into its branches. Under water, she could see the boat and kept on the far side of the sunken pine tree.

The boat rowed away. She rose, and breathed with a terrible caution.

For ten minutes he rowed back and forth where she had last been seen, searching through the water with his eyes for her body. The search was methodical and reasoned. Peering through the thick pine needles, she saw that he kept every part of the small lake's shore under constant watch. She could not have swum ashore undetected. He had made sure of the sapling. He patrolled the lake-surface. She did not break it. He could not but believe her dead. He had, in fact, seen her drown.

He rowed unhurriedly back toward the cottage, and

at the sight of his retreat she trembled so that she dared not cling to the sapling lest its shaking tell him of her presence behind it. He beached the boat. He went to the house. He entered it.

For a moment, Jane desperately contemplated a crazy dash for the farther lakeshore. But she was afraid.

There was silence. Stillness. Tranquillity. Jane clung to her green refuge in the middle of water. Insects shrilled contentedly in the sunlight. She prayed desperately for George Holloway to come quickly and drive away the man who had so resolutely and so ruthlessly attempted to murder her. . . .

Then George Holloway came out of the house. He carried the ax. Just as the other man had carried it. He put it away in the shed. He went to the lakeshore and took off his shoes and coat. He walked into the water—fully clothed—and deliberately soaked himself all over. Then he got into the boat and picked up the oars. He rowed out from the shore and resumed a search of the water for Jane's body, peering down everywhere.

Jane's brain was blank. It simply ceased to work. She was stupefied, and a yammering panic told her that she had gone mad. The man who had tried to murder her was George! But George had no reason to murder her! They were friends, not close friends, but surely on as good terms. He had been a guest at the cottage twice before. He was not a lunatic. If ever any man in the world thought coolly and cold-bloodedly about every action he performed, it was George Holloway. He might be capable of fierce passion, but he had nothing to gain by her death. But what did he want then?

He'd said he'd come early. He'd come first. He'd ransacked the house for garments in which to disguise himself. They were doubtless returned to where he'd found them. He'd arranged with absolute cunning that up to the very instant of her death he could always declare that he was playing a practical joke.

But he had no reason! He couldn't have done this! It was madness!

When the first motor car load of her guests drove out of the woods-road and called gaily to the empty cottage, Jane was a shivering, almost gibbering wreck. She saw George row in hastily to greet the newcomers. She saw him—soaking wet—explain anxiously. By his gestures, he said that when he arrived, the cottage was open and Jane vanished and the rowboat floated empty on the lake. He showed them something from the boat, her purse. Actually, she'd left it in the upstairs bedroom. He explained that he'd been uneasy, and had swum out to the boat. and that he'd been trying to find some trace of her in the water. . . .

The car whirled and went racketing back through the woods-road. It would be going for police, for someone to help search for Jane's drowned body. A second carload of guests arrived. George's pantomime was gone through again by the firstcomers, milling about in horror. George, himself, was seated on a log with his face in his hands.

Jane might, of course, have called from her place, but she was filled with such terror of George Holloway that she merely clung trembling to the sapling. It was not until two newcomers pushed the boat out into the lake again, and resumed a helpless search for her body, that she could even think of drawing attention to herself. Even then her voice would not carry. It was not until many fruitless trips back and forth had brought the rowboat near the planted sapling that she was able to give a croaking hail. And then she trembled violently when they came to her.

She was ghastly white. She twitched and chattered. Her story of the events leading up to the moment was incoherent. She knew that it was implausible. Her rescuers did not believe it. As they neared the boat, and agitated people crowded to see her returned from the dead, one of the two rescuers tapped his head significantly.

That made things worse. She was numb with horror when they lifted her ashore.

Then George Holloway approached, his face seemingly alight with relief. "Good Lord! Jane!" he cried feverishly. "I looked everywhere for you."

Jane found herself screaming shrilly. And then there was another car braking, and two men in uniform in it besides the girl who had driven frantically for help; and the police came forward and Jane clawed at them and gasped out her story again between whimperings of pure panic. And part of the panic came from doubt of her own sanity. She babbled.

"Now, now, lady," said one of the policemen. "You're all right now, anyhow. You get into bed and rest, and we'll talk to this guy and ask him why he tried to kill you."

They didn't believe it, either.

Jane sobbed. "He hadn't any reason," she said desperately. "That's it! He hadn't any reason! We've always been friends. Why, only last night I offered him a lift in the rain."

Then she stopped. Her hand went to her throat. Her eyes fixed upon George Holloway, and he was restrained and meticulous and impeccable even with his clothing still damp from the lake. And his manner was that of perfect composure and solicitude. But the skin of his face was going slowly whiter and whiter, until it was a queer shade of gray, and drops of sweat oozed out on his forehead.

"Last—last night," said Jane, struggling to speak past a vast lump in her throat, "I drove our maid home in the rain. I saw him at Mulberry and Haynes Streets at the stoplight. He was with a blonde girl, and they —were quarreling, and she was—crying. He—glared at me when I offered them a lift. And he—later he phoned me and asked me not to mention having seen him."

One of the cops jumped. The other turned his head sharply.

"Lady," said the second cop quietly. "You're wrong. He hadda reason. By the looks of him now, he knows I've guessed it. Y'see, lady, we found a blonde girl this mornin' not far from Mulberry an' Haynes. An' we wanted pretty bad to know who was with her last night. You see, some guy murdered her."

SIR ARTHUR CONAN DOYLE
(1859-1930)

. . . was born in Edinburgh, the grandson of a well-known political cartoonist and the nephew of the artist who created the famous cover for Punch *magazine.*

Like many other famous writers, Doyle started his career as a doctor. As a medical student at Edinburgh University, he was deeply impressed by one of his professors, a thin, wiry and very skillful surgeon, who could diagnose not only illness, but also his patients' occupations and character. Later, when Doyle started writing stories in order to supplement the meager earnings from his poor medical practice, he drew on his memories of this doctor to create Sherlock Holmes.

Holmes is, without doubt, the greatest fictional detective in all literature. His dry wit, his deceptively nonchalant manner, and, above all, his remarkable powers of analysis and deduction are enjoyed the world over. In the adventure of "The Engineer's Thumb," Holmes's superlatively rational observations provide a happy contrast to the gory events of the main narrative.

Sherlock Holmes explains

the murderous attack upon

THE ENGINEER'S THUMB

OF ALL the problems which have been submitted to my friend Mr. Sherlock Holmes for solution during the years of our intimacy, there were only two which I was the means of introducing to his notice—that of Mr. Hatherley's thumb, and that of Colonel Warburton's madness. Of these the latter may have afforded a finer field for an acute and original observer, but the other was so strange in its inception and so dramatic in its details that it may be the more worthy of being placed upon record, even if it gave my friend fewer openings for those deductive methods of reasoning by which he achieved such remarkable results. The story has, I believe, been told more than once in the newspapers, but, like all such narratives, its effect is much less striking when set forth *en bloc* in a single half-column of print than when the facts slowly evolve before your own eyes, and the mystery clears gradually away as each new discovery furnishes a step which leads on to the complete truth. At the time the circumstances made a deep impression upon me, and the lapse of two years has hardly served to weaken the effect.

It was in the summer of '89, not long after my marriage, that the events occurred which I am now about to summarize. I had returned to civil practice and had finally abandoned Holmes in his Baker Street rooms, although I continually visited him and occasionally even persuaded him to forego his Bohemian habits so far as to come and visit us. My practice had steadily increased, and as I happened to live at no very great distance from Paddington Station, I got a few patients from among the officials. One of these, whom I had cured of a painful and lingering disease, was never weary of advertising my virtues and of endeavoring to send me on every sufferer over whom he might have any influence.

One morning, at a little before seven o'clock, I was awakened by the maid tapping at the door to announce that two men had come from Paddington and were waiting in the consulting-room. I dressed hurriedly, for I knew by experience that railway cases were seldom trivial, and hastened downstairs. As I descended, my old ally, the guard, came out of the room and closed the door tightly behind him.

"I've got him here," he whispered, jerking his thumb

over his shoulder; "he's all right."

"What is it, then?" I asked, for his manner suggested that it was some strange creature which he had caged up in my room.

"It's a new patient," he whispered. "I thought I'd bring him round myself; then he couldn't slip away. There he is, all safe and sound. I must go now, Doctor; I have my dooties, just the same as you." And off he went, this trusty tout, without even giving me time to thank him.

I entered my consulting-room and found a gentleman seated by the table. He was quietly dressed in a suit of heather tweed, with a soft cloth cap which he had laid down upon my books. Round one of his hands he had a handkerchief wrapped, which was mottled all over with bloodstains. He was young, not more than five-and-twenty, I should say, with a strong, masculine face; but he was exceedingly pale and gave me the impression of a man who was suffering from some strong agitation, which it took all his strength of mind to control.

"I am sorry to call on you so early, Doctor," said he, "but I have had a very serious accident during the night. I came in by train this morning, and on inquiring at Paddington as to where I might find a doctor, a worthy fellow very kindly escorted me here. I gave the maid a card, but I see that she has left it upon the side-table."

I took it up and glanced at it. "Mr. Victor Hatherley, hydraulic engineer, 16A, Victoria Street (3d floor)." That was the name, style, and abode of my morning visitor. "I regret that I have kept you waiting," said I, sitting down in my library-chair. "You are fresh from a night journey, I understand, which is in itself a monotonous occupation."

"Oh, my night could not be called monotonous," said he, and laughed. He laughed very heartily, with a high, ringing note, leaning back in his chair and shaking his sides. All my medical instincts rose up against that laugh.

"Stop it!" I cried; "pull yourself together!" and I poured out some water from a carafe.

It was useless, however. He was off in one of those hysterical outbursts which come upon a strong nature when some great crisis is over and gone. Presently he came to himself once more, very weary and pale-looking.

"I have been making a fool of myself," he gasped.

"Not at all. Drink this." I dashed some brandy into the water, and the color began to come back to his bloodless cheeks.

"That's better!" said he. "And now, Doctor, perhaps you would kindly attend to my thumb, or rather to the place where my thumb used to be."

He unwound the handkerchief and held out his hand. It gave even my hardened nerves a shudder to look at it. There were four protruding fingers and a horrid red, spongy surface where the thumb should have been. It had been hacked or torn right out from the roots.

"Good heavens!" I cried, "this is a terribly injury. It must have bled considerably."

"Yes, it did. I fainted when it was done, and I think that I must have been senseless for a long time. When I came to I found that it was still bleeding, so I tied one end of my handkerchief very tightly round the wrist and braced it up with a twig."

"Excellent! You should have been a surgeon."

"It is a question of hydraulics, you see, and came within my own province."

"This has been done," said I, examining the wound, "by a very heavy and sharp instrument."

"A thing like a cleaver," said he.

"An accident, I presume?"

"By no means."

"What! a murderous attack?"

"Very murderous indeed."

"You horrify me."

I sponged the wound, cleaned it, dressed it, and finally covered it over with cotton wadding and carbolized bandages. He lay back without wincing, though he bit his lip from time to time.

"How is that?" I asked when I had finished.

"Capital! Between your brandy and your bandage, I feel a new man. I was very weak, but I have had a good deal to go through."

"Perhaps you had better not speak of the matter. It is evidently trying to your nerves."

"Oh, no, not now. I shall have to tell my tale to the police; but, between ourselves, if it were not for the convincing evidence of this wound of mine, I should be surprised if they believed my statement; for it is a very extraordinary one, and I have not much in the way of proof with which to back it up; and, even if they believe me, the clues which I can give them are so vague that it is a question whether justice will be done."

"Ha!" cried I, "if it is anything in the nature of a problem which you desire to see solved, I should strongly recommend you to come to my friend, Mr. Sherlock Holmes, before you go to the official police."

"Oh, I have heard of that fellow," answered my visitor, "and I should be very glad if he would take the matter up, though of course I must use the official police as well. Would you give me an introduction to him?"

"I'll do better. I'll take you round to him myself."

"I should be immensely obliged to you."

"We'll call a cab and go together. We shall just be in time to have a little breakfast with him. Do you feel equal to it?"

"Yes; I shall not feel easy until I have told my story."

"Then my servant will call a cab, and I shall be with you in an instant." I rushed upstairs, explained the matter shortly to my wife, and in five minutes was inside a hansom, driving with my new acquaintance to Baker Street.

Sherlock Holmes was, as I expected, lounging about his sitting-room in his dressing-gown, reading the agony column of *The Times* and smoking his before-breakfast pipe, which was composed of all the plugs and dottles left from his smokes of the day before, all carefully dried and collected on the corner of the mantlepiece. He received us in his quietly genial fashion, ordered fresh rashers and eggs, and joined us in a hearty meal. When it was concluded he settled our new acquaintance upon the sofa, placed a pillow beneath his head, and laid a glass of brandy and water within his reach.

"It is easy to see that your experience has been no common one, Mr. Hatherley," said he. "Pray, lie down there and make yourself absolutely at home. Tell us what you can, but stop when you are tired and keep up your strength with a little stimulant."

"Thank you," said my patient, "but I have felt another man since the doctor bandaged me, and I think that your breakfast has completed the cure. I shall take up as little of your valuable time as possible, so I shall start at once upon my peculiar experiences."

Holmes sat in his big armchair with the weary, heavy-lidded expression which veiled his keen and eager nature, while I sat opposite to him, and we listened in silence to the strange story which our visitor detailed to us.

"You must know," said he, "that I am an orphan and a bachelor, residing alone in lodgings in London. By profession I am a hydraulic engineer, and I have had considerable experience of my work during the seven years that I was apprenticed to Venner & Matheson, the well-known firm, of Greenwich. Two years ago, having served my time, and having also come into a fair sum of money through my poor father's death, I determined to start in business for myself and took professional chambers in Victoria Street.

"I suppose that everyone finds his first independent start in business a dreary experience. To me it has been exceptionally so. During two years I have had three consultations and one small job, and that is absolutely all that my profession has brought me. My gross takings amount to £27 10s. Every day, from nine in the morning until four in the afternoon, I waited in my little den, until at last my heart began to sink, and I came to believe that I should never have any practice at all.

"Yesterday, however, just as I was thinking of leaving the office, my clerk entered to say there was a gentleman waiting who wished to see me upon business. He brought up a card, too, with the name of 'Colonel Lysander Stark' engraved upon it. Close at his heels came the colonel himself, a man rather over the middle size, but of an exceeding thinness. I do not think that I have ever seen so thin a man. His whole face sharpened away into nose and chin, and the skin of his cheeks was drawn quite tense over his outstanding bones. Yet this emaciation seemed to be his natural habit, and due to no disease, for his eye was bright, his step brisk, and his bearing assured. He was plainly but neatly dressed, and his age, I should judge, would be nearer forty than thirty.

" 'Mr. Hatherley?' said he, with something of a

German accent. 'You have been recommended to me, Mr. Hatherley, as being a man who is not only proficient in his profession but is also discreet and capable of preserving a secret.'

"I bowed, feeling as flattered as any young man would at such an address. 'May I ask who it was who gave me so good a character?'

" 'Well, perhaps it is better that I should not tell you that just at this moment. I have it from the same source that you are both an orphan and a bachelor and are residing alone in London.'

" 'That is quite correct,' I answered; 'but you will excuse me if I say that I cannot see how all this bears upon my professional qualifications. I understand that it was on a professional matter that you wished to speak to me?'

" 'Undoubtedly so. But you will find that all I say is really to the point. I have a professional commission for you, but absolute secrecy is quite essential—*absolute* secrecy, you understand, and of course we may expect that more from a man who is alone than from one who lives in the bosom of his family.'

" 'If I promise to keep a secret,' said I, 'you may absolutely depend upon my doing so.'

"He looked very hard at me as I spoke, and it seemed to me that I had never seen so suspicious and questioning an eye.

" 'Do you promise, then?' said he at last.

" 'Yes, I promise.'

" 'Absolute and complete silence before, during, and

after? No reference to the matter at all, either in word or writing?'

" 'I have already given you my word.'

" 'Very good.' He suddenly sprang up, and darting like lightning across the room he flung open the door. The passage outside was empty.

" 'That's all right,' said he, coming back. 'I know the clerks are sometimes curious as to their master's affairs. Now we can talk in safety.' He drew up his chair very close to mine and began to stare at me again with the same questioning and thoughtful look.

"A feeling of repulsion, and of something akin to fear had begun to rise within me at the strange antics of this fleshless man. Even my dread of losing a client could not restrain me from showing my impatience.

" 'I beg that you will state your business, sir,' said I; 'my time is of value.' Heaven forgive me for that last sentence, but the words came to my lips.

" 'How would fifty guineas for a night's work suit you?' he asked.

" 'Most admirably.'

" 'I say a night's work, but an hour's would be nearer the mark. I simply want your opinion about a hydraulic stamping machine which has got out of gear. If you show us what is wrong we shall soon set it right ourselves. What do you think of such a commission as that?'

" 'The work appears to be light and the pay munificent.'

" 'Precisely so. We shall want you to come tonight

by the last train. That train will bring you to us.'

" 'Where to?'

" 'To Eyford, in Berkshire. It is a little place near the borders of Oxfordshire, and within seven miles of Reading. There is a train from Paddington which would bring you there at about 11:15.'

" 'Very good.'

" 'I shall come down in a carriage to meet you.'

" 'There is a drive, then?' I asked him.

" 'Yes, our little place is quite out in the country. It is a good seven miles from Eyford Station.'

" 'Then we can hardly get there before midnight. I suppose there would be no chance of a train back. I should be compelled to stop the night.'

" 'Yes, we could easily give you a shake-down.'

" 'That is very awkward. Could I not come at some more convenient hour?'

" 'We have judged it best that you should come late. It is to recompense you for any inconvenience that we are paying to you, a young and unknown man, a fee which would buy an opinion from the very heads of your profession. Still, of course, if you would like to draw out of the business, there is plenty of time to do so.'

"I thought of the fifty guineas, and of how very useful they would be to me. 'Not at all,' said I, 'I shall be very happy to accommodate myself to your wishes. I should like, however, to understand a little more clearly what it is that you wish me to do.'

" 'Quite so. It is very natural that the pledge of

secrecy which we have exacted from you should have
aroused your curiosity. I have no wish to commit you
to anything without your having it all laid before
you. I suppose that we are absolutely safe from eaves-
droppers?'

" 'Entirely.'

" 'Then the matter stands thus. You are probably
aware that fuller's-earth is a valuable product, and that
it is only found in one or two places in England?'

" 'I have heard so.'

" 'Some little time ago I bought a small place—a
very small place—within ten miles of Reading. I was
fortunate enough to discover that there was a deposit
of fuller's-earth in one of my fields. On examining it,
however, I found that this deposit was a comparatively
small one, and that it formed a link between two very
much larger ones upon the right and left—both of
them, however, in the grounds of my neighbors. These
good people were absolutely ignorant that their land
contained that which was quite as valuable as a gold-
mine. Naturally, it was to my interest to buy their land
before they discovered its true value, but unfortunately
I had no capital by which I could do this. I took a few
of my friends into the secret, however, and they suggested that we should quietly and secretly work our
own little deposit, and that in this way we should earn
the money which would enable us to buy the neighboring fields. This we have now been doing for some
time, and in order to help us in our operations we
erected a hydraulic press. This press, as I have already

explained, has got out of order, and we wish your advice upon the subject. We guard our secret very jealously, however, and if it once became known that we had hydraulic engineers coming to our little house, it would soon rouse inquiry, and then, if the facts came out, it would be good-bye to any chance of getting these fields and carrying out our plans. That is why I have made you promise me that you will not tell a human being that you are going to Eyford tonight. I hope that I make it all plain?'

" 'I quite follow you,' said I. 'The only point which I could not quite understand was what use you could make of a hydraulic press in excavating fuller's-earth, which, as I understand, is dug out like gravel from a pit.'

" 'Ah!' said he carelessly, 'we have our own process. We compress the earth into bricks, so as to remove them without revealing what they are. But that is a mere detail. I have taken you fully into my confidence now, Mr. Hatherley, and I have shown you how I trust you.' He rose as he spoke. 'I shall expect you, then, at Eyford at 11:15.'

" 'I shall certainly be there.'

" 'And not a word to a soul.' He looked at me with a last, long, questioning gaze, and then, pressing my hand in a cold, dank grasp, he hurried from the room.

"Well, when I came to think it all over in cool blood I was very much astonished, as you may both think, at this sudden commission which had been intrusted to me. On the one hand, of course, I was glad, for the fee was at least tenfold what I should have asked had I set a price upon my own services, and it was possible that this order might lead to other ones. On the other hand, the face and manner of my patron had made an unpleasant impression upon me, and I could not think that his explanation of the fuller's-earth was sufficient to explain the necessity for my coming at midnight, and his extreme anxiety lest I should tell anyone of my errand. However, I threw all fears to the winds, ate a hearty supper, drove to Paddington, and started off, having obeyed to the letter the injunction as to holding my tongue.

"At Reading I had to change not only my carriage but my station. However, I was in time for the last train to Eyford, and I reached the little dim-lit station after eleven o'clock. I was the only passenger who got out there, and there was no one upon the platform save a single sleepy porter with a lantern. As I passed out through the wicket gate, however, I found my acquaintance of the morning waiting in the shadow upon the other side. Without a word he grasped my arm and hurried me into a carriage, the door of which was standing open. He drew up the windows on either side, tapped on the wood-work, and away we went as fast as the horse could go."

"One horse?" interjected Holmes.

"Yes, only one."

"Did you observe the color?"

"Yes, I saw it by the side-lights when I was stepping into the carriage. It was a chestnut."

"Tired-looking or fresh?" Holmes asked.

"Oh, fresh and glossy."

"Thank you. I am sorry to have interrupted you. Pray continue your most interesting statement."

"Away we went then, and we drove for at least an hour. Colonel Lysander Stark had said that it was only seven miles, but I should think, from the rate that we seemed to go, and from the time that we took, that it must have been nearer twelve. He sat at my side in silence all the time, and I was aware, more than once when I glanced in his direction, that he was looking at me with great intensity. The country roads seem to be not very good in that part of the world, for we lurched and jolted terribly. I tried to look out of the windows to see something of where we were, but they were made of frosted glass, and I could make out nothing save the occasional bright blur of a passing light. Now and then I hazarded some remark to break the monotony of the journey, but the colonel answered only in monosyllables, and the conversation soon flagged. At last, however, the bumping of the road was exchanged for the crisp smoothness of a gravel-drive, and the carriage came to a stand. Colonel Lysander Stark sprang out, and, as I followed after him, pulled me swiftly into a porch which gaped in front of us. We stepped, as it were, right out of the carriage and into the hall, so that I failed to catch the most fleeting glance of the front of the house. The instant that I had crossed the threshold the door slammed heavily behind us, and I heard faintly the rattle of the wheels as the carriage drove away. After that there was no sound at all.

"It was pitch dark inside the house, and the colonel fumbled about looking for matches and muttering under his breath. Suddenly a door opened at the other end of the passage, and a long, golden bar of light shot out in our direction. It grew broader, and a woman appeared with a lamp in her hand, which she held above her head, pushing her face forward and peering at us. I could see that she was pretty, and from the gloss with which the light shone upon her dark dress I knew that it was a rich material. She spoke a few words in a foreign tongue in a tone as though asking a question, and when my companion answered in a gruff monosyllable she gave such a start that the lamp nearly fell from her hand. Colonel Stark went up to her, whispered something in her ear, and then, pushing her back into the room from whence she had come, he walked towards me again with the lamp in his hand.

"'Perhaps you will have the kindness to wait in this room for a few minutes,' said he, throwing open another door. It was a quiet, little, plainly furnished room, with a round table in the centre, on which several German books were scattered. Colonel Stark laid down the lamp on the top of a harmonium beside the door. 'I shall not keep you waiting an instant,' said he, and vanished into the darkness.

"I glanced at the books upon the table, and in spite of my ignorance of German I could see that two of them were treatises on science, the others being volumes of poetry. Then I walked across to the window,

hoping that I might catch some glimpse of the countryside, but an oak shutter, heavily barred, was folded
across it. It was a wonderfully silent house. There was
an old clock ticking loudly somewhere in the passage,
but otherwise everything was deadly still. A vague
feeling of uneasiness began to steal over me. Who were
these German people, and what were they doing living
in this strange, out-of-the-way place? And where was
the place? I was ten miles or so from Eyford, that was
all I knew, but whether north, south, east, or west I had
no idea. For that matter, Reading, and possibly other
large towns, were within that radius, so the place might
not be so secluded, after all. Yet it was quite certain,
from the absolute stillness, that we were in the country.
I paced up and down the room, humming a tune under
my breath to keep up my spirits and feeling that I was
thoroughly earning my fifty-guinea fee.

"Suddenly, without any preliminary sound in the
midst of the utter stillness, the door of my room swung
slowly open. The woman was standing in the aperture,
the darkness of the hall behind her, the yellow light
from my lamp beating upon her eager and beautiful
face. I could see at a glance that she was sick with fear,
and the sight sent a chill to my own heart. She held up
one shaking finger to warn me to be silent, and she
shot a few whispered words of broken English at me,
her eyes glancing back, like those of a frightened horse,
into the gloom behind her.

" 'I would go,' said she, trying hard, as it seemed to
me, to speak calmly; 'I would go. I should not stay

here. There is no good for you to do.'

" 'But, madam,' said I, 'I have not yet done what I came for. I cannot possibly leave until I have seen the machine.'

" 'It is not worth your while to wait,' she went on. 'You can pass through the door; no one hinders.' And then, seeing that I smiled and shook my head, she suddenly threw aside her constraint and made a step forward, with her hands wrung together. 'For the love of Heaven!' she whispered, 'get away from here before it is too late!'"

"But I am somewhat headstrong by nature, and the more ready to engage in an affair when there is some obstacle in the way. I thought of my fifty-guinea fee, of my wearisome journey, and of the unpleasant night which seemed to be before me. Was it all to go for nothing? Why should I slink away without having carried out my commission, and without the payment which was my due? This woman might, for all I knew, be a monomaniac. With a stout bearing, therefore, though her manner had shaken me more than I cared to confess, I still shook my head and declared my intention of remaining where I was. She was about to renew her entreaties when a door slammed overhead, and the sound of several footsteps was heard upon the stairs. She listened for an instant, threw up her hands with a despairing gesture, and vanished as suddenly and as noiselessly as she had come.

"The newcomers were Colonel Lysander Stark and a short thick man with a chinchilla beard growing out of the creases of his double chin, who was introduced to me as Mr. Ferguson.

" 'This is my secretary and manager,' said the colonel. 'By the way, I was under the impression that I left this door shut just now. I fear that you have felt the draught.'

" 'On the contrary,' said I, 'I opened the door myself because I felt the room to be a little close.'

"He shot one of his suspicious looks at me. 'Perhaps we had better proceed to business, then,' said he. 'Mr. Ferguson and I will take you up to see the machine.'

" 'I had better put my hat on, I suppose.'

" 'Oh, no, it is in the house.'

" 'What, you dig fuller's-earth in the house?'

" 'No, no. This is only where we compress it. But never mind that. All we wish you to do is to examine the machine and to let us know what is wrong with it.'

"We went upstairs together, the colonel first with the lamp, the fat manager and I behind him. It was a labyrinth of an old house, with corridors, passages, narrow winding staircases, and little low doors, the thresholds of which were hollowed out by the generations who had crossed them. There were no carpets and no signs of any furniture above the ground floor, while the plaster was peeling off the walls, and the damp was breaking through in green, unhealthy blotches. I tried to put on as unconcerned an air as possible, but I had not forgotten the warnings of the lady, even though I disregarded them, and I kept a keen eye upon my two companions. Ferguson appeared to be a morose and silent man, but I could see from the little that he said that he was at least a fellow-countryman.

"Colonel Lysander Stark stopped at last before a low door, which he unlocked. Within was a small, square room, in which the three of us could hardly get at one time. Ferguson remained outside, and the colonel ushered me in.

" 'We are now,' said he, 'actually within the hydraulic press, and it would be a particularly unpleasant thing for us if anyone were to turn it on. The ceiling of this small chamber is really the end of the descending piston, and it comes down with the force of many tons upon this metal floor. There are small lateral columns of water outside which receive the force, and which transmit and multiply it in the manner which is familiar to you. The machine goes readily enough, but there is some stiffness in the working of it, and it has lost a little of its force. Perhaps you will have the goodness to look it over and to show us how we can set it right.'

"I took the lamp from him, and I examined the machine very thoroughly. It was indeed a gigantic one, and capable of exercising enormous pressure. When I passed outside, however, and pressed down the levers which controlled it, I knew at once by the whishing sound that there was a slight leakage, which allowed a regurgitation of water through one of the side cylinders. An examination showed that one of the India-rubber bands which was round the head of a driving-rod had shrunk so as not quite to fill the socket along which it worked. This was clearly the cause of the loss of power, and I pointed it out to my companions, who followed my remarks very carefully and asked several particular questions as to how they should proceed to set it right. When I had made it clear to them, I returned to the main chamber of the machine and took a good look at it to satisfy my own curiosity. It was obvious at a glance that the story of the fuller's-earth was the merest fabrication, for it would be absurd to suppose that so powerful an engine could be designed for so inadequate a purpose. The walls were of wood, but the floor consisted of a large iron trough, and when I came to examine it I could see a crust of metallic deposit all over it. I had stooped and was scraping at this to see exactly what it was when I heard a muttered exclamation in German and saw the cadaverous face of the colonel looking down at me.

" 'What are you doing there?' he asked.

"I felt angry at having been tricked by so elaborate a story as that which he had told me. 'I was admiring your fuller's-earth,' said I; 'I think that I should be better able to advise you as to your machine if I knew what the exact purpose was for which it was used.'

"The instant that I uttered the words I regretted the rashness of my speech. His face set hard, and a baleful light sprang up in his gray eyes.

" 'Very well,' said he, 'you shall know all about the machine.' He took a step backward, slammed the little door, and turned the key in the lock. I rushed towards it and pulled at the handle, but it was quite secure, and did not give in the least to my kicks and shoves.

'Hello!' I yelled. 'Hello! Colonel! Let me out!'

"And then suddenly in the silence I heard a sound which sent my heart into my mouth. It was the clank of the levers and the swish of the leaking cylinder. He had set the engine at work. The lamp still stood upon the floor where I had placed it when examining the trough. By its light I saw that the black ceiling was coming down upon me, slowly, jerkily, but, as none knew better than myself, with a force which must within a minute grind me to a shapeless pulp. I threw myself, screaming, against the door, and dragged with my nails at the lock. I implored the colonel to let me out, but the remorseless clanking of the levers drowned my cries. The ceiling was only a foot or two above my head, and with my hand upraised I could feel its hard, rough surface. Then it flashed through my mind that the pain of my death would depend very much upon the position in which I met it. If I lay on my face the weight would come upon my spine, and I shuddered to think of that dreadful snap. Easier the other way, perhaps; and yet, had I the nerve to lie and look up at that deadly black shadow wavering down upon me? Already I was unable to stand erect, when my eye caught something which brought a gush of hope back to my heart.

"I have said that though the floor and ceiling were of iron, the walls were of wood. As I gave a last hurried glance around, I saw a thin line of yellow light between two of the boards, which broadened and broadened as a small panel was pushed backward. For an instant I could hardly believe that here was indeed a door which led away from death. The next instant I threw myself through, and lay half-fainting upon the other side. The panel had closed again behind me, but the crash of the lamp, and a few moments afterwards the clang of the two slabs of metal, told me how narrow had been my escape.

"I was recalled to myself by a frantic plucking at my wrist, and I found myself lying upon the stone floor of a narrow corridor, while a woman bent over me and tugged at me with her left hand, while she held a candle in her right. It was the same good friend whose warning I had so foolishly rejected.

" 'Come! come!' she cried breathlessly. 'They will be here in a moment. They will see that you are not there. Oh, do not waste the so-precious time, but come!'

"This time, at least, I did not scorn her advice. I staggered to my feet and ran with her along the corridor and down a winding stair. The latter led to another broad passage, and just as we reached it we heard the sound of running feet and the shouting of two voices, one answering the other from the floor on which we were and from the one beneath. My guide stopped and looked about her like one who is at her wit's end. Then she threw open a door which led into a bedroom, through the window of which the moon was shining brightly.

" 'It is your only chance,' she said. 'It is high, but it may be that you can jump it.'

"As she spoke a light sprang into view at the further

end of the passage, and I saw the lean figure of Colonel Lysander Stark rushing forward with a lantern in one hand and a weapon like a butcher's cleaver in the other. I rushed across the bedroom, flung open the window, and looked out. How quiet and sweet and wholesome the garden looked in the moonlight, and it could not be more than thirty feet down. I clambered out upon the sill, but I hesitated to jump until I should have heard what passed between my savior and the ruffian who pursued me. If she were ill-used, then at any risks I was determined to go back to her assistance. The thought had hardly flashed through my mind before he was at the door, pushing his way past her; but she threw her arms round him and tried to hold him back.

" 'Fritz! Fritz!' she cried in English, 'remember your promise after the last time. You said it should not be again. He will be silent! Oh, he will be silent!'

" 'You are mad, Elise!' he shouted, struggling to break away from her. 'You will be the ruin of us. He has seen too much. Let me pass, I say!' He dashed her to one side, and, rushing to the window, cut at me with his heavy weapon. I had let myself go, and was hanging by the hands to the sill, when his blow fell. I was conscious of a dull pain, my grip loosened, and I fell into the garden below.

"I was shaken but not hurt by the fall; so I picked myself up and rushed off among the bushes as hard as I could run, for I understood that I was far from being out of danger yet. Suddenly, however, as I ran, a deadly dizziness and sickness came over me. I glanced down at my hand, which was throbbing painfully, and then, for the first time, saw that my thumb had been cut off and that the blood was pouring from my wound. I endeavored to tie my handkerchief round it, but there came a sudden buzzing in my ears, and next moment I fell in a dead faint among the rose-bushes.

"How long I remained unconscious I cannot tell. It must have been a very long time, for the moon had sunk, and a bright morning was breaking when I came to myself. My clothes were all sodden with dew, and my coat sleeve was drenched with blood from my wounded thumb. The smarting of it recalled in an instant all the particulars of my night's adventure, and I sprang to my feet with the feeling that I might hardly yet be safe from my pursuers. But to my astonishment, when I came to look round me, neither house nor garden was to be seen. I had been lying in an angle of the hedge close by the highroad, and just a little lower down was a long building, which proved, upon my approaching it, to be the very station at which I had arrived upon the previous night. Were it not for the ugly wound upon my hand, all that had passed during those dreadful hours might have been an evil dream.

"Half dazed, I went into the station and asked about the morning train. There would be one to Reading in less than an hour. The same porter was on duty, I found, as had been there when I arrived. I inquired of him whether he had ever heard of Colonel Lysander Stark. The name was strange to him. Had he observed a carriage the night before waiting for me? No, he had not. Was there a police-station anywhere near? There was one about three miles off.

"It was too far for me to go, weak and ill as I was. I determined to wait until I got back to town before telling my story to the police. It was a little past six when I arrived, so I went first to have my wound dressed, and then the doctor was kind enough to bring me along here. I put the case into your hands and shall do exactly what you advise."

We both sat in silence for some little time after listening to this extraordinary narrative. Then Sherlock Holmes pulled down from the shelf one of the ponderous commonplace books in which he placed his cuttings.

"Here is an advertisement which will interest you," said he. "It appeared in all the papers about a year ago. Listen to this:

> Lost, on the 9th inst., Mr. Jeremiah Hayling, aged twenty-six, a hydraulic engineer. Left his lodgings at ten o'clock at night, and has not been heard of since. Was dressed in—

etc., etc. Ha! That represents the last time the the colonel needed to have his machine overhauled, I fancy."

"Good heavens!" cried my patient. "Then that explains what the girl said."

"Undoubtedly. It is quite clear that the colonel was a cool and desperate man, who was absolutely determined that nothing should stand in the way of his little game, like those out-and-out pirates who will leave no survivor from a captured ship. Well, every moment now is precious, so if you feel equal to it we shall go down to Scotland Yard at once as a preliminary to starting for Eyford."

Some three hours or so afterwards we were all in the train together, bound from Reading to the little Berkshire village. There were Sherlock Holmes, the hydraulic engineer, Inspector Bradstreet, of Scotland Yard, a plain-clothes man, and myself. Bradstreet had spread an ordnance map of the county out upon the seat and was busy with his compasses drawing a circle with Eyford for its centre.

"There you are," said he. "That circle is drawn at a radius of ten miles from the village. The place we want must be somewhere near that line. You said ten miles, I think, sir."

"It was an hour's good drive."

"And you think that they brought you back all that way when you were unconscious?"

"They must have done so. I have a confused memory, too, of having been lifted and conveyed somewhere."

"What I cannot understand," said I, "is why they should have spared you when they found you lying fainting in the garden. Perhaps the villain was softened by the woman's entreaties."

"I hardly think that likely. I never saw a more inexorable face in my life."

"Oh, we shall soon clear up all that," said Bradstreet. "Well, I have drawn my circle, and I only wish I knew at what point upon it the folk that we are in search of are to be found. It's quite a wide area to search."

"I think I could lay my finger on it," said Holmes.

"Really, now!" cried the inspector, "you have formed your opinion! Come, now, we shall see who agrees with you. I say it is south, for the country is more deserted there."

"And I say east," said my patient.

"I am for west," remarked the plain-clothes man. "There are several quiet little villages up there."

"And I am for north," said I, "because there are no hills there, and our friend says that he did not notice the carriage go up any."

"Come," cried the inspector, laughing; "it's a very pretty diversity of opinion. We have boxed the compass among us. Who do you give your casting vote to?"

"You are all wrong."

"But we can't *all* be."

"Oh, yes, you can. This is my point." He placed his finger in the centre of the circle. "This is where we shall find them."

"But the twelve-mile drive?" gasped Hatherley.

"Six out and six back. Nothing simpler. You say yourself that the horse was fresh and glossy when you got in. How could it be that if it had gone twelve miles over heavy roads?"

"Indeed, it is a likely ruse enough," observed Bradstreet thoughtfully. "Of course there can be no doubt as to the nature of this gang."

"None at all," said Holmes. "They are coiners on a large scale, and have used the machine to form the amalgam which has taken the place of silver."

"We have known for some time that a clever gang was at work," said the inspector. "They have been turning out half-crowns by the thousand. We even traced them as far as Reading, but could get no farther, for they had covered their traces in a way that showed that they were very old hands. But now, thanks to this lucky chance, I think that we have got them right enough."

But the inspector was mistaken, for those criminals were not destined to fall into the hands of justice. As we rolled into Eyford Station we saw a gigantic column of smoke which streamed up from behind a small clump of trees in the neighborhood and hung like an immense ostrich feather over the landscape.

"A house on fire?" asked Bradstreet as the train steamed off again on its way.

"Yes, sir!" said the station-master.

"When did it break out?"

"I hear that it was during the night, sir, but it has got worse, and the whole place is in a blaze."

"Whose house is it?"

"Dr. Becher's."

"Tell me," broke in the engineer, "is Dr. Becher a German, very thin, with a long, sharp nose?"

The station-master laughed heartily. "No, sir, Dr. Becher is an Englishman, and there isn't a man in the parish who has a better-lined waistcoat. But he has a gentleman staying with him, a patient, as I understand, who is a foreigner, and he looks as if a little good Berkshire beef would do him no harm."

The station-master had not finished his speech before we were all hastening in the direction of the fire. The road topped a low hill, and there was a great widespread whitewashed building in front of us, spouting fire at every chink and window, while in the garden in front three fire-engines were vainly striving to keep the flames under.

"That's it!" cried Hatherley, in intense excitement. "There is the gravel-drive, and there are the rose-bushes where I lay. That second window is the one that I jumped from."

"Well, at least," said Holmes, "you have had your revenge upon them. There can be no question that it was your oil-lamp which, when it was crushed in the press, set fire to the wooden walls, though no doubt they were too excited in the chase after you to observe it at the time. Now keep your eyes open in this crowd for your friends of last night, though I very much fear that they are a good hundred miles off by now."

And Holmes's fears came to be realized, for from that day to this no word has ever been heard either of the beautiful woman, the sinister German, or the morose Englishman. Early that morning a peasant had met a cart containing several people and some very bulky boxes driving rapidly in the direction of Reading, but there all traces of the fugitives disappeared, and even Holmes's ingenuity failed ever to discover the least clue as to their whereabouts.

The firemen had been much perturbed at the strange arrangements which they had found within, and still more so by discovering a newly severed human thumb upon a window-sill of the second floor. About sunset, however, their efforts were at last successful, and they subdued the flames, but not before the roof had fallen in, and the whole place been reduced to such absolute ruin that, save some twisted cylinders and iron piping, not a trace remained of the machinery which had cost our unfortunate acquaintance so dearly. Large masses of nickel and of tin were discovered stored in an out-house, but no coins were to be found, which may have explained the presence of those bulky boxes which have been already referred to.

How our hydraulic engineer had been conveyed from the garden to the spot where he recovered his senses might have remained forever a mystery were it not for the soft mould, which told us a very plain tale. He had evidently been carried down by two persons, one of whom had remarkably small feet and the other unusually large ones. On the whole, it was most prob-able that the silent Englishman, being less bold or less murderous than his companion, had assisted the woman to bear the unconscious man out of the way of danger.

"Well," said our engineer ruefully as we took our seats to return once more to London, "it has been a pretty business for me! I have lost my thumb and I have lost a fifty-guinea fee, and what have I gained?"

"Experience," said Holmes, laughing. "Indirectly it may be of value, you know; you have only to put it into words to gain the reputation of being excellent company for the remainder of your existence."

Sherlock Holmes diagnosed

THE SPECKLED BAND

to be a vicious, lethal weapon

IT WAS EARLY in April in the year '83 that I woke one morning to find Sherlock Holmes standing, fully dressed, by the side of my bed. He was a late riser, as a rule, and as the clock on the mantelpiece showed me that it was only a quarter-past seven, I blinked up at him in some surprise, and perhaps just a little resentment, for I was myself regular in my habits.

"Very sorry to wake you up, Watson," said he, "but it's the common lot this morning. Mrs. Hudson has been awakened, she retorted upon me, and I on you."

"What is it, then—a fire?"

"No; a client. It seems that a young lady has arrived in a considerable state of excitement, who insists upon seeing me. She is waiting now in the sitting room."

I had no keener pleasure than in following Holmes in his professional investigations, and in admiring the rapid deductions, as swift as intuitions, and yet always founded on a logical basis, with which he unraveled the problems which were submitted to him. I rapidly threw on my clothes and was ready in a few minutes to accompany my friend down to the sitting room. A lady dressed in black and heavily veiled, who had been sitting in the window, rose as we entered.

"Good morning, madam," said Holmes cheerily. "My name is Sherlock Holmes. This is my intimate friend and associate, Dr. Watson, before whom you can speak as freely as before myself. Ha! I am glad to see that Mrs. Hudson has had the good sense to light the fire. Pray draw up to it, and I shall order you a cup of hot coffee, for I observe that you are shivering."

"It is not cold which makes me shiver," said the woman in a low voice, changing her seat as requested.

"What, then?"

"It is fear, Mr. Holmes. It is terror." She raised her veil as she spoke, and we could see that she was indeed in a pitiable state of agitation, her face all drawn and gray, with restless, frightened eyes, like those of some hunted animal.

"You must not fear," said he soothingly, bending forward and patting her forearm. "We shall soon set matters right, I have no doubt. You have come in by train this morning, I see."

"You know me, then?"

"No, but I observe the second half of a return ticket in the palm of your left glove. You must have started early, and yet you had a good drive in a dog cart, along heavy roads, before you reached the station."

The lady gave a violent start and stared in bewilderment at my companion.

"There is no mystery, my dear madam," said he, smiling. "The left arm of your jacket is spattered with mud in no less than seven places. The marks are perfectly fresh. There is no vehicle save a dog cart which throws up mud in that way, and then only when you sit on the left-hand side of the driver."

"Whatever your reasons may be, you are perfectly correct," said she. "I started from home before six, reached Leatherhead at twenty past, and came in by the first train to Waterloo. Sir, I can stand this strain no longer; I shall go mad if it continues. I have no one to turn to—none, save only one, who cares for me, and he, poor fellow, can be of little aid.

"I have heard of you, Mr. Holmes; I have heard of you from Mrs. Farintosh, whom you helped in the hour of her sore need."

"Farintosh," said he. "Ah yes, I recall the case; it was concerned with an opal tiara. I think it was before your time, Watson. I can only say, madam, that I shall be happy to devote the same care to your case as I did to that of your friend. As to reward, my profession is its own reward; but you are at liberty to defray whatever expenses I may be put to, at the time which suits you best. And now I beg that you will lay before us everything that may help us in forming an opinion upon the matter."

"My name is Helen Stoner, and I am living with my stepfather, who is the last survivor of one of the oldest Saxon families in England, the Roylotts of Stoke Moran, on the western border of Surrey."

Holmes nodded his head. "The name is familiar to me," said he.

"The family was at one time among the richest in England. In the last century, however, four successive heirs were of a dissolute and wasteful disposition, and the family ruin was eventually completed by a gambler in the days of the Regency. Nothing was left save a few acres of ground, and the two-hundred-year-old house, which is itself crushed under a heavy mortgage.

"The last squire dragged out his existence there, living the horrible life of an aristocratic pauper; but his only son, my stepfather, seeing that he must adapt himself to the new conditions, obtained an advance from a relative, which enabled him to take a medical degree and went out to Calcutta, where, by his professional skill and his force of character, he established a large practice. In a fit of anger, however, caused by some robberies which had been perpetrated in the house, he beat his native butler to death and narrowly escaped a capital sentence. As it was, he suffered a long term of imprisonment and afterwards returned to England a morose and disappointed man.

"When Dr. Roylott was in India he married my mother, Mrs. Stoner, the young widow of Major-General Stoner, of the Bengal Artillery. My sister Julia and I were twins, and we were only two years old at the time of my mother's re-marriage. She had a considerable sum of money—and this she bequeathed to Dr. Roylott entirely while we resided with him, with a provision that a certain annual sum should be allowed to each of us in the event of our marriage. Shortly after our return to England my mother died—she was killed eight years ago in a railway accident near Crewe. Dr. Roylott then took us to live with him in the old ancestral house at Stoke Moran. The money which my mother had left was enough for all our wants, and there seemed to be no obstacle to our happiness.

"But a terrible change came over our stepfather about this time. Instead of making friends and exchanging visits with our neighbors, who had at first been overjoyed to see a Roylott of Stoke Moran back in the old family seat, he shut himself up in his house and seldom came out save to indulge in ferocious quarrels with whoever might cross his path.

"Violence of temper approaching to mania has been hereditary in the men of the family, and in my stepfather's case it had, I believe, been intensified by his long residence in the tropics. A series of disgraceful brawls took place, two of which ended in the police court, until at last he became the terror of the village, and the folks would fly at his approach, for he is a man of immense strength, and absolutely uncontrollable in his anger.

"He had no friends at all save the wandering gyp-

sies, and he would give these vagabonds leave to en-
camp upon the few acres of bramble-covered land
which represent the family estate. He has a passion
also for Indian animals, which are sent over to him by
a correspondent, and he has at this moment a cheetah
and a baboon, which wander freely over his grounds
and are feared by the villagers almost as much as is their
master.

"You can imagine from what I say that my poor
sister Julia and I had no great pleasure in our lives.
No servant would stay with us, and for a long time we
did all the work of the house. She was but thirty at the
time of her death, and yet her hair had already begun
to whiten, even as mine has."

"Your sister is dead, then?"

"She died just two years ago, and it is of her death
that I wish to speak to you. You can understand that,
living the life which I have described, we were little
likely to see anyone of our own age and position. We
had, however, an aunt who lives near Harrow. Julia
went there at Christmas two years ago, and met there
a major· in the Marines, to whom she became engaged. My stepfather learned of the engagement when
my sister returned and offered no objection to the
marriage; but within a fortnight of the day which had
been fixed for the wedding, the terrible event occurred
which has deprived me of my only companion."

Sherlock Holmes had been leaning back in his chair
with his eyes closed and his head sunk in a cushion,
but he half opened his lids now and glanced across at

his visitor. He wanted to hear everything.

"Pray be precise as to details," said he.

"It is easy for me to be so, for every event of that dreadful time is seared into my memory. The manor house is, as I have already said, very old, and only one wing is now inhabited. The bedrooms in this wing are on the ground floor, the sitting rooms being in the central block of the buildings. Of these bedrooms the first is Dr. Roylott's, the second my sister's, and the third my own. There is no communication between them, but they all open out into the same corridor. Do I make myself plain?"

"Perfectly so."

"The windows of the three rooms open out upon the lawn. That fatal night my sister came into my room because she was troubled by the smell of Dr. Roylott's cigar. She sat for some time, chatting about her approaching wedding. At eleven o'clock she rose to leave me, but she paused at the door and looked back.

"'Tell me, Helen,' said she, 'have you ever heard anyone whistle in the dead of the night?'

"'Never,' said I.

"'I suppose that you could not possibly whistle, yourself, in your sleep?'

"'Certainly not. But why?'

"'Because during the last few nights I have always, about three in the morning, heard a low, clear whistle. I thought that I would just ask you whether you had heard it.'

"'No, I have not. It must be those wretched gypsies.'

" 'Well, it is of no great consequence, at any rate.' She smiled back at me, closed my door, and a few moments later I heard her key turn in the lock."

"Indeed," said Holmes. "Was it your custom always to lock yourselves in at night?"

"Always."

"And why?"

"I think that I mentioned to you that the doctor kept a cheetah and a baboon. We had no feeling of security unless our doors were locked."

"Quite so. Pray proceed with your statement."

"I could not sleep that night. A vague feeling of impending misfortune impressed me. My sister and I, you will recollect, were twins, and you know how subtle are the links which bind two souls which are so closely allied. It was a wild night. The wind was howling outside, and the rain was beating and splashing against the windows. Suddenly, amid all the hubbub of the gale, there burst forth the wild scream of a terrified woman. I knew that it was my sister's voice. I sprang from my bed, wrapped a shawl round me, and rushed to the door.

"As I entered the corridor, I seemed to hear a low whistle, such as my sister had described, and a few moments later a clanging sound, as if a mass of metal had fallen. As I ran down the passage, I saw that my sister's door was unlocked, and revolved slowly upon its hinges. I stared at it horror-stricken, not knowing what was about to issue from it. By the light of the corridor lamp I saw my sister appear at the opening, her face blanched with terror, her hands groping for help, her whole figure swaying to and fro like that of a drunkard.

"I ran to her and threw my arms around her, but at that moment her knees seemed to give way and she fell to the ground. She writhed as one who is in terrible pain, and her limbs were dreadfully convulsed. At first I thought that she had not recognized me, but as I bent over her she suddenly shrieked out in a voice which I shall never forget, 'Oh, my God! Helen! It was the band! The speckled band!'

"There was something else which she would fain have said, and she stabbed with her finger into the air in the direction of the doctor's room, but a fresh convulsion seized her and choked her words. I rushed out, calling loudly for my stepfather, and I met him hastening from his room in his dressing gown. When he reached my sister's side she was unconscious, and though he poured brandy down her throat and sent for medical aid from the village, all efforts were in vain, for she slowly sank and died without having recovered her consciousness. Such was the dreadful end of my beloved sister."

"One moment," said Holmes, "are you sure about this whistle and metallic sound? Could you swear to it?"

"That was what the county coroner asked me at the inquiry. It is my strong impression that I heard it, and yet, among the crash of the gale and the creaking of an old house, I may possibly have been deceived."

"Was your sister dressed?"

"No, she was in her nightdress. In her right hand

was found the charred stump of a match, and in her left a match box."

"Showing that she had struck a light and looked about her when the alarm took place. That is important. And what conclusions did the coroner come to?"

"He investigated the case with great care, for Dr. Roylott's conduct had long been notorious in the county, but he was unable to find any satisfactory cause of death. My evidence showed that the door had been fastened upon the inner side, and the windows were blocked by old-fashioned shutters with broad iron bars, which were secured every night.

"The walls were carefully sounded and were shown to be quite solid all round, and the flooring was also thoroughly examined, with the same result. The chimney is wide, but is barred up by four large staples. It is certain, therefore, that my sister was quite alone when she met her end. Besides, there were no marks of any violence upon her."

"How about poison?"

"The doctors examined her for it, but without success."

"Were there gypsies on the plantation at the time?"

"Yes, there are nearly always some there."

"Ah, and what did you gather from this allusion to a band—a speckled band?"

"Sometimes I have thought that it was merely the wild talk of delirium; sometimes that it may have referred to some band of people, perhaps to these very gypsies on the plantation. I do not know whether the spotted handkerchiefs which so many of them wear over their heads might have suggested the strange adjective which she used."

Holmes shook his head like a man who is far from being satisfied.

"These are very deep waters," said he; "pray go on with your narrative."

"Two years have passed since then, and my life has been until lately lonelier than ever. A month ago, however, a dear friend, whom I have known for many years, did me the honor to ask my hand in marriage and we are to be married in the spring.

"Two days ago some repairs were started in the west wing of the building, and my bedroom wall was pierced, so that I have had to move into the chamber in which my sister died, and to sleep in the very bed in which she slept. Imagine, then, my thrill of terror when last night, as I lay awake, thinking over her terrible fate, I suddenly heard in the silence of the night the low whistle which had been the herald of her own death. I sprang up and lit the lamp, but nothing was to be seen in the room.

"I was too shaken to go to bed again, however, so I dressed, and as soon as it was daylight I slipped out, got a dog-cart at the Crown Inn, which is opposite, and drove to Leatherhead, from whence I have come on this morning with the one object of seeing you and asking your advice."

"You have done wisely," said my friend. "But have you told me all?"

"Why, what do you mean? What is it?"

For answer Holmes pushed back the frill of black lace which fringed the hand that lay upon our visitor's knee. Five little livid spots, the marks of four fingers and a thumb, were printed upon the white wrist.

"You have been cruelly used," said Holmes.

The lady colored deeply and covered over her injured wrist. "He is a hard man," she said, "and perhaps, he hardly knows his own strength."

There was a long silence, during which Holmes leaned his chin upon his hands and stared into the crackling fire.

"This is a very deep business," he said at last. "There are a thousand details which I should desire to know before I decide upon our course of action. Yet we have not a moment to lose. If we were to come to Stoke Moran today, would it be possible for us to look over these rooms without the knowledge of your stepfather?"

"As it happens, he spoke of coming into town today upon some most important business. It is probable that he will be away all day."

"Excellent. You are not averse to this trip, Watson?"

"By no means."

"Then we shall both come. What are you going to do yourself?"

"I have one or two things which I would wish to do now that I am in town. But I shall return by the twelve o'clock train, so as to be there in time for your coming."

"And you may expect us early in the afternoon. I have myself some small business matters to attend to. Will you not wait and breakfast?"

"No, I must go. My heart is lightened already since I have confided my trouble to you. I shall look forward to seeing you again this afternoon." She dropped her thick black veil over her face and softly glided from the room.

"And what do you think of it all, Watson?" asked Sherlock Holmes, leaning back in his chair.

"It seems to me to be a most dark and sinister business."

"Dark enough and sinister enough."

"Yet if the lady is correct in saying that the flooring and walls are sound, and that the door, window, and chimney are impassable, then her sister must undoubtedly have been alone when she met her mysterious end."

"What becomes, then, of these nocturnal whistles, and what of the very peculiar words of the dying woman?" mused Holmes.

"I cannot think."

"When you combine the ideas of whistles at night, the presence of a band of gypsies who are on intimate terms with this old doctor, the fact that we have every reason to believe that the doctor has an interest in preventing his stepdaughter's marriage, the dying allusion to a band, and, finally, the fact that Miss Helen Stoner heard a metallic clang, which might have been caused by one of those metal bars that secured the shutters falling back into its place, I think that these factors all point to a theory that may help clear the mystery."

"But what, then, did the gypsies do?" I asked quickly.

"I cannot imagine," Holmes responded thoughtfully. "It is precisely for that reason that we are going to Stoke Moran this day. I want to see for myself whether there are any fatal objections to my theory. Only a spot investigation will tell me what I want to know. — But what in the name of the devil!"

The ejaculation had been drawn from my companion by the fact that our door had been suddenly dashed open, and that a huge man had framed himself in the aperture. His costume was a peculiar mixture of the professional and of the agricultural, having a black top-hat, a long frock-coat, and a pair of high gaiters, with a hunting crop swinging in his hand. So tall was he that his hat actually brushed the cross bar of the doorway, and his breadth seemed to span it across from side to side. A large face, seared with a thousand wrinkles, burned yellow with the sun, and marked with every evil passion, was turned from one to the other of us, while his deep-set, bile-shot eyes, and his high, thin, fleshless nose, gave him somewhat the resemblance to a fierce old bird of prey.

"Which of you is Holmes?" asked this apparition.

"My name, sir; but you have the advantage of me," said my companion quietly.

"I am Dr. Grimesby Roylott, of Stoke Moran."

"Indeed, Doctor," said Holmes blandly. "Pray take a seat."

"I will do nothing of the kind. My stepdaughter has been here. I have traced her. What has she been saying to you?"

"It is a little cold for this time of year," said Holmes.

"What has she been saying to you?" screamed the old man furiously.

"But I have heard that the crocuses promise well," continued my companion inperturbably.

"Ha! You put me off, do you?" said our new visitor, taking a step forward and shaking his hunting crop. "I know you, you scoundrel! I have heard of you before. You are Holmes, the meddler."

My friend smiled.

"Holmes, the busybody!"

His smile broadened.

"Holmes, the Scotland Yard Jack-in-office!"

Holmes chuckled heartily. "Your conversation is most entertaining," said he. "When you go out close the door, for there is a decided draught."

"I will go when I have said my say. Don't you dare to meddle with my affairs. I know that Miss Stoner has been here. I traced her! I am a dangerous man to fall foul of! See here." He stepped swiftly forward, seized the poker, and bent it into a curve with his huge brown hands.

"See that you keep yourself out of my grip," he snarled, and hurling the twisted poker into the fireplace he strode out of the room.

"He seems a very amiable person," said Holmes, laughing. "I am not quite so bulky, but if he had remained I might have shown him that my grip was not much more feeble than his own." As he spoke he picked up the steel poker and, with a sudden effort, straightened it out again.

"Fancy his having the insolence to confound me with the official detective force! This incident gives zest to our investigation, however, and I only trust that our little friend will not suffer from her imprudence in allowing this brute to trace her. And now, Watson, we shall order breakfast, and afterwards I shall walk down to Doctors' Commons, where I hope to get some data which may help us in this matter."

It was nearly one o'clock when Sherlock Holmes returned from his excursion. He held in his hand a sheet of blue paper, scrawled over with notes and figures.

"I have seen the will of the deceased wife," said he. "Each daughter can claim an income in case of marriage. It is evident, therefore, that if both girls had married, this beauty would have had a mere pittance, while even one of them would cripple him to a very serious extent. My morning's work has not been wasted, since it has proved that he has the very strongest motives for standing in the way of anything of the sort.

"And now, Watson, this is too serious for dawdling, especially as the old man is aware that we are interesting ourselves in his affairs; so if you are ready, we shall call a cab and drive to Waterloo. I should be very much obliged if you would slip your revolver into your pocket. An Eley's No. 2 is an excellent argument with gentlemen who can twist steel pokers into knots. That and a toothbrush are, I think, all that we need."

At Waterloo we were fortunate in catching a train for Leatherhead, where we hired a trap at the station inn and drove for four or five miles through the lovely Surrey lanes. It was a perfect day, with a bright sun and a few fleecy clouds in the heavens. The trees and wayside hedges were just throwing out their first green shoots, and the air was full of the pleasant smell of the moist earth. To me at least there was a strange contrast between the sweet promise of the spring and this sinister quest upon which we were engaged. My companion sat in the front of the trap, his arms folded, his hat pulled down over his eyes, and his chin sunk upon his breast, buried in the deepest thought. Suddenly, however, he started, tapped me on the shoulder, and pointed over the meadows.

"Look there!" said he.

A heavily timbered park stretched up in a gentle slope, thickening into a grove at the highest point. From amid the branches there jutted out the gray gables and high rooftops of a very old mansion.

"Stoke Moran?" Holmes asked the driver.

"Yes, sir, that be the house of Dr. Grimesby Roylott," remarked the driver.

"There is some building going on there," said Holmes; "that is where we are going."

"There's the village," said the driver, pointing to a

cluster of roofs some distance to the left; "but if you want to get to the house, you'll find it shorter to get over this stile, and go by the footpath over the fields. There it is, where the lady is walking."

"And the lady, I fancy, is Miss Stoner," observed Holmes, shading his eyes. "Yes, I think we had better do as you suggest."

We got off, paid our fare, and the trap rattled back on its way to Leatherhead.

"I thought it as well," said Holmes as we climbed the stile, "that this fellow should think we had come here as architects, or on some definite business. It may stop his gossip. Good afternoon, Miss Stoner. You see that we have been as good as our word."

Our client of the morning had hurried forward to meet us with a face which spoke her joy. "I have been waiting so eagerly for you," she cried, shaking hands with us warmly. "All has turned out splendidly. Dr. Roylott has gone to town, and it is unlikely that he will be back before evening."

"We have had the pleasure of making the doctor's acquaintance," said Holmes, and in a few words he sketched out what had occurred. Miss Stoner turned white to the lips as she listened.

"Good heavens!" she cried, "he has followed me, then."

"So it appears."

"He is so cunning that I never know when I am safe from him. What will he say when he returns?"

"He must guard himself, for he may find that there

is someone more cunning than himself upon his track. You must lock yourself up from him tonight. If he is violent, we shall take you away to your aunt's at Harrow. Now, we must make the best use of our time, so kindly take us at once to the rooms which we are to examine."

The building was of gray, lichen-blotched stone, with a high central portion and two curving wings, like the claws of a crab, thrown out on each side. In one of these wings the windows were broken and blocked with wooden boards, while the roof was partly caved in, a picture of ruin. The central portion was in little better repair, but the right-hand block was comparatively modern, and the blinds in the windows, with the blue smoke curling up from the chimneys, showed that this was where the family resided. Some scaffolding had been erected against the end wall, and the stone work had been broken into, but there were no signs of any workmen at the moment of our visit. Holmes walked slowly up and down the ill-trimmed lawn and examined with deep attention the outsides of the windows.

"This, I take it, belongs to the room in which you used to sleep, the center one to your sister's, and the one next to the main building to Dr. Roylott's chamber?"

"Exactly so. But I am now sleeping in the middle one."

"Pending the alterations, as I understand. By the way, there does not seem to be any very pressing need for repairs at that end wall."

"There were none. I believe that it was an excuse to move me from my room."

"Ah! that is suggestive. Now, on the other side of this narrow wing runs the corridor from which these three rooms open. There are windows in it, of course?"

"Yes, but very small ones. Too narrow for anyone to pass through."

"As you both locked your doors at night, your rooms were unapproachable from that side. Now, would you have the kindness to go into your room and bar your shutters?"

Miss Stoner did so, and Holmes, after a careful examination through the open window, endeavoured in every way to force the shutter open, but without success. There was no slit through which a knife could be passed to raise the bar. Then with his lens he tested the hinges, but they were of solid iron, built firmly into the massive masonry. "Hum!" said he, scratching his chin in some perplexity, "my theory certainly presents some difficulties. No one could pass through these shutters if they were bolted. Well, we shall see if the inside throws any light upon the matter."

A small side door led into the whitewashed corridor from which the three bedrooms opened. Holmes refused to examine the third chamber, so we passed at once to the second, that in which Miss Stoner was now sleeping, and in which her sister had met with her fate. It was a homely little room, with a low ceiling and a gaping fireplace, after the fashion of old country houses. A brown chest of drawers stood in one corner, a narrow white-counterpaned bed in another, and a dressing table on the left-hand side of the window. These articles, with two small wickerwork chairs, made up all the furniture in the room save for a square of Wilton carpet in the center. The boards round and the panelling of the walls were of brown, worm-eaten oak, so old and discoloured that it may have dated from the original building of the house. Holmes drew one of the chairs into a corner and sat silent, while his eyes travelled round and round and up and down, taking in every detail of the room.

"Where does that bell communicate with?" he asked at last, pointing to a thick bell-rope which hung down beside the bed, the tassel actually lying upon the pillow.

"It goes to the housekeeper's room."

"It looks newer than the òther things?"

"Yes, it was only put there a couple of years ago."

"Your sister asked for it, I suppose?"

"No, I never heard of her using it. We used always to get what we wanted for ourselves."

"Indeed, it seemed unnecessary to put so nice a bell-pull there. You will excuse me for a few minutes while I satisfy myself as to this floor." He threw himself down upon his face with his lens in his hand and crawled swiftly backward and forward, examining minutely the cracks between the boards. Then he did the same with the woodwork with which the chamber was panelled. Finally he walked over to the bed and spent some time in staring at it and in running his eye up and down the wall. Finally he took the bell-rope in his hand and gave it a brisk tug.

"Why, it's a dummy," said he.

"Won't it ring?"

"No, it is not even attached to a wire. This is very interesting. You can see now that it is fastened to a hook just above where the little opening for the ventilator is."

"How very absurd! I never noticed that before."

"Very strange!" muttered Holmes, pulling at the rope. "There are one or two very singular points about this room. For example, what a fool a builder must be to open a ventilator into another room, when, with the same trouble, he might have placed the ventilator so as to communicate with the outside air!"

"That is also quite modern," said the lady.

"Done about the same time as the bell-rope?" remarked Holmes.

"Yes, there were several little changes carried out about that time."

"They seem to have been of a most interesting character—dummy bell-ropes, and ventilators which do not ventilate. With your permission, Miss Stoner, we shall now carry our researches into the inner apartment."

Dr. Grimesby Roylott's chamber was larger than that of his stepdaughter, but was as plainly furnished. A camp bed, a small wooden shelf full of books, mostly of a technical character, an armchair beside the bed, a plain wooden chair against the wall, a round table, and a large iron safe were the principal things which met the eye. Holmes walked slowly round and examined each of them with the keenest interest.

"What's in here?" he asked, tapping the safe.

"My stepfather's business papers."

"There isn't a cat in it, for example?"

"No. What a strange idea!"

"Well, look at this!" He took up a small saucer of milk which stood on the top of it.

"No; we don't keep a cat. But there is a cheetah and a baboon."

"Ah, yes, of course! Well, a cheetah is just a big cat, and yet a saucer of milk does not go very far in satisfying its wants, I daresay. There is one point which I should wish to determine." He squatted down in front of the wooden chair and examined the seat of it with the greatest attention.

"Thank you. That is quite settled," said he, rising and putting his lens in his pocket. "Hello! Here is something interesting!"

The object which had caught his eye was a small dog lash hung on one corner of the bed. The lash, however, was curled upon itself and tied so as to make a loop of whipcord.

"What do you make of that, Watson?"

"It's a common enough lash. But I don't know why it should be tied."

"That is not quite so common, is it? Ah, me! It's a wicked world, and when a clever man turns his brains to crime it is the worst of all. I think that I have seen enough now, Miss Stoner, and with your permission we shall walk out upon the lawn."

I had never seen my friend's face so grim or his brow so dark as it was when we turned from the scene of this investigation. We had walked several times up and down the lawn, neither Miss Stoner nor myself liking to break in upon his thoughts before he roused himself from his reverie.

"It is very essential, Miss Stoner," said he, "that you should absolutely follow my advice in every respect."

"I shall most certainly do so."

"The matter is too serious for any hesitation. Your life may depend upon your compliance."

"I assure you that I am in your hands."

"In the first place, both my friend and I must spend the night in your room."

Both Miss Stoner and I gazed at him in astonishment.

"Yes, it must be so. Let me explain. I believe that that is the village inn over there?"

"Yes, that is the 'Crown'," answered Miss Stoner.

"Very good. Your windows would be visible from there?"

"Certainly."

"You must confine yourself to your room, on pretense of a headache when your stepfather comes back. Then when you hear him retire for the night, you must open the shutters of your window, undo the hasp, put your lamp there as a signal to us, and then withdraw quietly with everything which you are likely to want into the room which you used to occupy."

"But what will you do?"

"We shall spend the night in your room, and we shall investigate the cause of this noise which has disturbed you."

"I believe, Mr. Holmes, that you have already made up your mind," said Miss Stoner, laying her hand upon my companion's sleeve.

"Perhaps I have."

"Then, for pity's sake, tell me what was the cause of my sister's death."

"I should prefer to have clearer proofs before I speak."

"You can at least tell me whether my own thought is correct, and if she died from some sudden fright."

"No, I do not think so. I think that there was probably some more tangible cause. And now, Miss Stoner, we must leave you, for if Dr. Roylott returned and saw us our journey would be in vain. Good-bye, and be brave; for if you will do what I have told you, you may rest assured that we shall soon drive away the dangers that threaten you."

Sherlock Holmes and I had no difficulty in engaging a bedroom and sitting room at the Crown Inn. They were on the upper floor, and from our window we could command a view of the avenue gate, and of the inhabited wing of Stoke Moran Manor House. At dusk we saw Dr. Grimesby Roylott drive past, his huge form looming up beside the little figure of the lad who drove him. The boy had some slight difficulty in undoing the heavy iron gates, and we heard the hoarse roar of the doctor's voice and saw the fury with which he shook his clenched fists at him. The trap drove on, and a few minutes later we saw a sudden light spring up among the trees as the lamp was lit in one of the sitting rooms.

"Do you know, Watson," said Holmes as we sat together in the gathering darkness, "I have really some scruples as to taking you tonight. There is a distinct element of danger."

"Can I be of assistance?"

"Your presence might be invaluable."

"Then I shall certainly come."

"It is very kind of you."

"You speak of danger. You have evidently seen more in these rooms than was visible to me."

"No, but I fancy that I may have deduced a little more. I imagine that you saw all that I did."

"I saw nothing remarkable save the bell-rope, and what purpose that could answer I confess is more than I can imagine."

"You saw the ventilator, too?"

"Yes, but I do not think that it is such a very unusual thing to have a small opening between two rooms. It was so small that a rat could hardly pass through."

"I knew that we should find a ventilator before ever we came to Stoke Moran."

"My dear Holmes!"

"Oh, yes, I did. You remember in her statement she said that her sister could smell Dr. Roylott's cigar.

Now, of course that suggested at once that there must be a communication between the two rooms. It could only be a small one, or it would have been remarked upon at the coroner's inquiry. I deduced a ventilator."

"But what harm can there be in that?"

"Well, there is at least a curious coincidence of dates. A ventilator is made, a cord is hung, and a lady who sleeps in the bed dies. Does not that strike you?"

"I cannot as yet see any connection."

"Did you observe anything very peculiar about that bed?"

"No."

"It was clamped to the floor. Did you ever see a bed fastened like that before?"

"I cannot say that I have," I acknowledged.

"The lady could not move her bed. It must always be in the same relative position to the ventilator and to the rope—for so we may call it, since it was clearly never meant for a bell-pull."

"Holmes," I cried, "I seem to see dimly what you are hinting at. We are only just in time to prevent some subtle and horrible crime."

"Subtle enough and horrible enough. When a doctor does go wrong he is the first of criminals. He has nerve and he has knowledge. Palmer and Pritchard were among the heads of their profession. This man strikes even deeper, but I think, Watson, that we shall be able to strike deeper still. But we shall have horrors enough before the night is over; for goodness' sake let us have a quiet pipe and turn our minds for a few hours to something more cheerful."

About nine o'clock the light among the trees was extinguished, and all was dark in the direction of the Manor House. Two hours passed slowly away, and then, suddenly, just at the stroke of eleven, a single bright light shone out right in front of us.

"That is our signal," said Holmes, springing to his feet; "it comes from the middle window."

As we passed out he exchanged a few words with the landlord, explaining that we were going on a late visit to an acquaintance, and that it was possible that we might spend the night there. A moment later we were out on the dark road, a chill wind blowing in our faces, and one yellow light twinkling in front of us through the gloom to guide us on our somber errand.

There was little difficulty in entering the grounds, for unrepaired breaches gaped in the old park wall. Making our way among the trees, we reached the lawn, crossed it, and were about to enter through the window when out from a clump of laurel bushes there darted what seemed to be a hideous and distorted child, who threw itself upon the grass with writhing limbs and then ran swiftly across the lawn into the darkness.

"My God!" I whispered; "did you see it?"

Holmes was for the moment as startled as I. His hand closed like a vise upon my wrist in his agitation. Then he broke into a low laugh and put his lips to my ear.

"It is a nice household," he murmured. "That is the baboon."

I had forgotten the strange pets which the doctor affected. There was a cheetah, too; perhaps we might find it upon our shoulders at any moment. I confess that I felt easier in my mind when, after following Holmes's example and slipping off my shoes, I found myself inside the bedroom. My companion noiselessly closed the shutters, moved the lamp onto the table, and cast his eyes round the room. All was as we had seen it in the daytime. Then creeping up to me and making a trumpet of his hand, he whispered into my ear so gently that it was all that I could do to distinguish the words, "The least sound would be fatal to our plans."

I nodded to show that I had heard.

"We must sit without light. He would see it through the ventilator."

I nodded again.

"Do not go asleep; your very life may depend upon it. Have your pistol ready in case we should need it. I will sit on the side of the bed, and you in that chair."

I took out my revolver and laid it on the table.

Holmes had brought up a long thin cane, and this he placed upon the bed beside him. By it he laid the box of matches and the stump of a candle. Then he turned down the lamp, and we were left in darkness.

How shall I ever forget that dreadful vigil? I could not hear a sound, not even the drawing of a breath, and yet I knew that my companion sat open-eyed, within a few feet of me, in the same state of nervous tension in which I was myself. The shutters cut off the least ray of light, and we waited in absolute darkness. From outside came the occasional cry of a night bird, and once at our very window a long-drawn catlike whine, which told us that the cheetah was indeed at liberty. Far away we could hear the deep tones of the parish clock, which boomed out every quarter of an hour. How long they seemed, those quarters! Twelve struck, and one and two and three, and still we sat waiting silently for whatever might befall.

Suddenly there was the momentary gleam of a light up in the direction of the ventilator, which vanished immediately, but was succeeded by a strong smell of burning oil and heated metal. Someone in the next room had lit a dark-lantern. I heard a gentle sound of movement, and then all was silent once more, though the smell grew stronger. For half an hour I sat with straining ears. Then suddenly another sound became audible—a very gentle, soothing sound, like that of a small jet of steam escaping continually from a kettle. The instant that we heard it, Holmes sprang from the bed, struck a match, and lashed furiously with his cane at the bell-pull.

"You see it, Watson?" he yelled. "You see it?"

But I saw nothing. At the moment when Holmes struck the light I heard a low, clear whistle, but the sudden glare flashing into my weary eyes made it impossible for me to tell what it was at which my friend lashed so savagely. I could, however, see that his face was deadly pale and filled with horror and loathing.

He had ceased to strike and was gazing up at the ventilator when suddenly there broke from the silence of the night the most horrible cry to which I have ever listened. It swelled up louder and louder, a hoarse yell of pain and fear and anger all mingled in the one dreadful shriek. They say that way down in the village, and even in the distant parsonage, that cry raised the sleepers from their beds. It struck cold to our hearts, and I stood gazing at Holmes, and he at me, until the last echoes of it had died away into the silence from which it rose.

"What can it mean?" I gasped.

"It means that it is all over," Holmes answered. "And perhaps, after all, it is for the best. Take your pistol, and we will enter Dr. Roylott's room."

With a grave face he lit the lamp and led the way down the corridor. Twice he struck at the chamber door without any reply from within. Then he turned the handle and entered, I at his heels, with the cocked pistol in my hand.

It was a singular sight which met my eyes. On the table stood a dark-lantern with the shutter half open, throwing a brilliant beam of light upon the iron safe, the door of which was ajar. Beside this table, on the wooden chair, sat Dr. Grimesby Roylott, clad in a long gray dressing gown, his bare ankles protruding beneath, and his feet thrust into red heelless Turkish slippers. Across his lap lay the short stock with the long lash which we had noticed during the day. His chin was cocked upward and his eyes were fixed in a dreadful, rigid stare at the corner of the ceiling. Round his brow he had a peculiar yellow band, with brownish speckles, which seemed to be bound tightly round his head. As we entered he made neither sound nor motion.

"The band! The speckled band!" whispered Holmes.

I took a step forward. In an instant his strange head-gear began to move, and there reared itself from among his hair the squat diamond-shaped head and puffed neck of a loathsome serpent.

"It is a swamp adder!" cried Holmes, "the deadliest snake in India. He has died within ten seconds of being bitten. Violence does, in truth, recoil upon the violent, and the schemer falls into the pit which he digs for another. Let us thrust this creature back into its den, and we can then remove Miss Stoner to some place of shelter and let the county police know what has happened."

As he spoke he drew the dog whip swiftly from the dead man's lap, and throwing the noose round the reptile's neck he drew it from its horrid perch and, carrying it at arm's length, threw it into the iron safe, which he closed upon it.

Such are the true facts of the death of Dr. Grimesby Roylott, of Stoke Moran. It is not necessary that I should prolong a narrative which has already run to too great a length by telling how we broke the sad news to the terrified girl, how we conveyed her by the morning train to the care of her good aunt at Harrow, of how the slow process of official inquiry came to the conclusion that the doctor met his fate while indiscreetly playing with a dangerous pet. The little which I had yet to learn of the case was told me by Sherlock Holmes as we travelled back next day.

"I had," said he, "come to an entirely erroneous conclusion; which shows, my dear Watson, how dangerous it always is to reason from insufficient data. The presence of the gypsies, and the word 'band,' used by the poor girl, no doubt to explain that which she had caught a hurried glimpse of by the light of her match, were sufficient to put me upon an entirely wrong scent. I can only claim the merit that I instantly reconsidered my position when it became clear to me that whatever danger threatened an occupant of the room, could not come in from either the door or the window. I then sought other evidence.

"My attention was speedily drawn, as I have already remarked to you, to this ventilator, and to the bell-rope which hung down to the bed. The discovery that this was a dummy, and that the bed was clamped to the floor, instantly gave rise to the suspicion that the rope was there as a bridge for something passing through the hole and coming to the bed. The idea of a snake instantly occurred to me, and when I coupled it with my knowledge that the doctor was furnished with a supply of creatures from India, I felt that I was probably on the right track.

"The idea of using a form of poison which could not possibly be discovered by any chemical test was just such a one as would occur to a clever and ruthless man who had had an Eastern training. The rapidity with which such a poison would take effect would also, from his point of view, be an advantage. It would be a sharp-eyed coroner, indeed, who could distinguish the two little dark punctures which would show where the poison fangs had done their work.

"Then I thought of the whistle. Of course he must recall the snake before the morning light revealed it to the victim. He had trained it, probably by the use of the milk which we saw, to return to him when summoned. He would put it through this ventilator at the hour that he thought best, with the certainty that it would crawl down the rope and land on the bed. It might or might not bite the occupant, perhaps she might escape every night for a week, but sooner or later she must fall a victim.

"I had come to these conclusions before ever I had entered his room. An inspection of his chair showed me that he had been in the habit of standing on it, which of course would be necessary in order that he should reach the ventilator. The sight of the safe, the saucer of milk, and the loop of whipcord were enough to finally dispel any doubts which may have remained. The metallic clang heard by Miss Stoner was obviously caused by her stepfather hastily closing the door of his safe upon its terrible occupant. Having once made up my mind, you know the steps which I took in order to put the matter to the proof. I heard the creature hiss, as I have no doubt that you did also, and I instantly lit the light and attacked it."

"With the result of driving it through the ventilator."

"And also with the result of causing it to turn upon its master at the other side. Some of the blows of my cane came home and roused its snakish temper, so that it flew upon the first person it saw. In this way, I am no doubt indirectly responsible for Dr. Grimesby Roylott's death, and I cannot say that it is likely to weigh very heavily upon my conscience."

W. W. JACOBS

. . . was born in London in 1863 and began his career as a clerk in the British Post Office. In his spare time, he started writing stories and articles. Three years after his first book was published, he quit his government post to devote his full time to writing. Aside from his short stories, Jacobs is best known for his plays, most of them one-act comedies. He died in London in 1943, a few days before his eightieth birthday.

Christopher Morley called him "one of the most permanently delightful short story writers who ever lived," and J. B. Priestly has hailed him as "a most finished, conscientious and delicate artist."

"The Monkey's Paw," perhaps Jacobs' best known work, is considered a classic—a masterpiece of suspense and terror.

Wishes came true with

THE MONKEY'S PAW

and death came too!

WITHOUT, the night was cold and wet, but in the small parlor of Lakesnam Villa the blinds were drawn and the fire burned brightly. Father and son were at chess; the former, who possessed ideas about the game involving radical changes, putting his king into such sharp and unnecessary perils that it even provoked comment from the whitehaired old lady knitting placidly by the fire.

"Hark at the wind," said Mr. White, who, having seen a fatal mistake after it was too late, was amiably desirous of preventing his son from seeing it.

"I'm listening," said the latter, grimly surveying the board as he stretched out his hand. "Check."

"I should hardly think that he'd come tonight," said

his father, with his hand poised over the board.

"Mate," replied the son.

"That's the worst of living so far out," bawled Mr. White, with sudden and unlooked-for violence; "of all the beastly, slushy, out-of-the-way places to live in, this is the worst. Pathway's a bog, and the road's a torrent. I don't know what people are thinking about. I suppose because only two houses on the road are let, they think the road doesn't matter."

"Never mind, dear," said his wife soothingly; "perhaps you'll win the next one."

Mr. White looked up sharply, just in time to intercept a knowing glance between mother and son. The words died on his lips, and he hid a guilty grin in his thin gray beard.

"There he is," said Herbert White, as the gate banged to loudly, and heavy footsteps came toward the door.

The old man rose with hospitable haste, and opening the door, was heard condoling with the new arrival. The new arrival also condoled with himself, so that Mrs. White said, "Tut, tut!" and coughed gently as her husband entered the room, followed by a tall, burly man, beady of eye and rubicund of visage.

"Sergeant Major Morris," Mr. White announced.

The sergeant major shook hands, and taking the proffered seat by the fire, watched contentedly while his host got out whisky and tumblers and stood a small copper kettle on the fire.

At the third glass his eyes got brighter, and he began to talk; the little family circle regarding with eager interest this visitor from distant parts, as he squared his broad shoulders in the chair and spoke of strange scenes and doughty deeds, of wars and plagues and strange peoples.

"Twenty-one years of it," said Mr. White, nodding at his wife and son. "When he went away he was a slip of a youth in the warehouse. Now look at him."

"He don't look to have taken much harm," said Mrs. White politely.

"I'd like to go to India myself," said the old man, "just to look around a bit, you know."

"Better where you are," said the sergeant major, shaking his head. He put down the empty glass and, sighing softly, shook it again.

"I should like to see those old temples and fakirs and jugglers," said the old man. "What was that you started telling me the other day about a monkey's paw or something, Morris?"

"Nothing," said the soldier hastily. "Leastways, nothing worth hearing."

"Monkey's paw?" said Mrs. White curiously.

"Well, it's just a bit of what you might call magic, perhaps," said the sergeant major offhandedly.

His three listeners leaned forward eagerly. The visitor absent-mindedly put his empty glass to his lips and then set it down again. His host filled it for him.

"To look at," said the sergeant major, fumbling in his pocket, "it's just an ordinary little paw, dried to a mummy."

He took something out of his pocket and proffered

it. Mrs. White drew back with a grimace, but her son, taking it, examined it curiously.

"And what is there special about it?" inquired Mr. White, as he took it from his son and, having examined it, placed it upon the table.

"It had a spell put on it by an old fakir," said the sergeant major, "a very holy man. He wanted to show that fate ruled people's lives, and that those who interfered with it did so to their sorrow. He put a spell on it so that three separate men could each have three wishes from it."

His manner was so impressive that his hearers were conscious that their light laughter jarred somewhat.

"Well, why don't you have three, sir?" said Herbert White cleverly.

The soldier regarded him in the way that middle age is wont to regard presumptuous youth. "I have," he said quietly, and his blotchy face whitened.

"And did you really have the three wishes granted?" asked Mrs. White.

"I did," said the sergeant major, and his glass tapped against his strong teeth.

"And has anybody else wished?" inquired the old lady.

"The first man had his three wishes, yes," was the reply. "I don't know what the first two were, but the third was for death. That's how I got the paw."

His tones were so grave that a hush fell upon the group. "If you've had your three wishes, it's no good to you now, then, Morris," said the old man at last.

"What do you keep it for? Why do you want it?"

The soldier shook his head. "Fancy, I suppose," he said slowly. "I did have some idea of selling it, but I don't think I will. It has caused enough mischief already. Besides, people won't buy. They think it's a fairy tale, some of them, and those who do think anything of it want to try it first and pay me afterward."

"If you could have another three wishes," said the old man, eyeing him keenly, "would you have them?"

"I don't know," said the other. "I don't know."

He took the paw, and dangling it between his front finger and thumb, suddenly threw it upon the fire. White, with a slight cry, stooped down and snatched it off.

"Better let it burn," said the soldier solemnly.

"If you don't want it, Morris," said the old man, "give it to me."

"I won't," said his friend doggedly. "I threw it on the fire. If you keep it, don't blame me for what happens. Pitch it on the fire again, like a sensible man."

The other shook his head and examined his new possession closely. "How do you do it?" he inquired.

"Hold it up in your right hand and wish aloud," said the sergeant major, "but I warn you of the consequences."

"Sounds like *The Arabian Nights*," said Mrs. White, as she rose and began to set the supper. "Don't you think you might wish for four pairs of hands for me?"

Her husband drew the talisman from his pocket and then all three burst into laughter as the sergeant major, with a look of alarm on his face, caught him by the arm. "If you must wish," he said gruffly, "wish for something sensible."

Mr. White dropped it back into his pocket, and placing chairs, motioned his friend to the table. In the business of supper the talisman was partly forgotten, and afterward the three sat listening in an enthralled fashion to a second installment of the soldier's adventures in India.

"If the tale about the monkey paw is not more truthful than those he has been telling us," said Herbert, as the door closed behind their guest, just in time for him to catch the last train, "we shan't make much out of it."

"Did you give him anything for it, father?" inquired Mrs. White, regarding her husband closely.

"A trifle," said he, coloring slightly. "He didn't want it, but I made him take it. And he pressed me again to throw it away."

"Likely!" said Herbert, with pretended horror. "Why, we're going to be rich, and famous, and happy. Wish to be an emperor, father, to begin with; then you can't be henpecked."

He darted round the table, pursued by the maligned Mrs. White armed with an antimacassar.

Mr. White took the paw from his pocket and eyed it dubiously. "I don't know what to wish for, and that's a fact," he said slowly. "It seems to me I've got all I want."

"If you only cleared the house, you'd be quite happy, wouldn't you?" said Herbert, putting his hand on his father's shoulder. "Well, wish for two hundred pounds, then; that will just do it, won't it?"

His father, smiling shamefacedly at his own credulity, held up the talisman, as his son, with a solemn face somewhat marred by a wink at his mother, sat down at the piano and struck a few impressive chords.

"I wish for two hundred pounds," said the old man distinctly.

A fine crash from the piano greeted the words, interrupted by a shuddering cry from the old man. His wife and son ran toward him.

"It moved," he cried, with a glance of disgust at the object as it lay on the floor. "As I wished it twisted in my hands like a snake."

"Well, I don't see the money," said his son, as he picked the paw up and placed it on the table, "I bet I never shall."

"It must have been your fancy, father," said his wife, regarding him anxiously.

He shook his head. "Never mind, though; there's no harm done, but it gave me a shock all the same."

They sat down by the fire again, while the two men finished their pipes. Outside, the wind was higher than ever, and the old man started nervously at the sound of a door banging upstairs. A silence unusual and depressing settled upon all three, which lasted until the old couple rose to retire for the night.

"I expect you'll find the cash tied up in a big bag in the middle of your bed," said Herbert, as he bade them good night, "and something horrible squatting upon the top of the wardrobe, watching you as you pocket your ill-gotten gains."

Next morning in the brightness of the wintry sun as it streamed over the breakfast table, Herbert laughed at his fears. There was an air of prosaic wholesomeness about the room, which it had lacked on the previous night, and the dirty, shriveled little paw was pitched on the sideboard with a carelessness which betokened no great belief in its virtues.

"I suppose all old soldiers are the same," said Mrs. White. "The idea of our listening to such nonsense! How could wishes be granted in these days? And if they could, how could two hundred pounds hurt you, father?"

"Might drop on his head from the sky," said the frivolous Herbert.

"Morris said the things happened so naturally," said his father, "that you might, if you so wished, attribute it to coincidence."

"Well, don't break into the money before I come back," said Herbert, as he rose from the table. "I'm afraid it'll turn you into a mean, avaricious man, and we shall have to disown you."

His mother laughed, and followed him to the door; watched him down the road, and returning to the breakfast table, was very happy at the expense of her husband's credulity. All of which did not prevent her from scurrying to the door at the postman's knock; nor did it prevent her from referring somewhat shortly to retired sergeant majors of bibulous habits, when she found that the post brought a tailor's bill.

"Herbert will have some more of his funny remarks, I expect, when he comes home," she said, as they sat at dinner.

"I dare say," said Mr. White, pouring himself out some beer; "but for all that, the thing moved in my hand; that I'll swear to."

"You thought it did," said the old lady soothingly.

"I say it did," replied the other. "There was no thought about it. I had just—What's the matter?"

His wife made no reply. She was watching the mysterious movements of a man outside, who, peering in an undecided fashion at the house, appeared to be trying to make up his mind to enter. Still mentally associated with the two hundred pounds, she noticed that the stranger was well dressed and wore a silk hat of glossy newness.

Three times he paused at the gate, and then walked on again. The fourth time he stood with his hand upon the gate, and then with sudden resolution flung it open and walked up the path. Mrs. White placed her hands behind her, and hurriedly unfastening the strings of her apron, put that useful article of apparel beneath the cushion of her chair.

She brought the stranger, who seemed ill at ease, into the room. He gazed furtively at Mrs. White, and listened in a preoccupied fashion as the old lady apologized for the appearance of the room, and her husband's coat, a garment which he usually reserved for the garden. She then waited as patiently as her sex would permit for him to broach his business, but he was at first strangely silent.

"I—was asked to call," he said at last, and stooped and picked a piece of cotton from his trousers. "I've come from Maw and Meggins."

The old lady started. "Is anything the matter?" she asked breathlessly. "Has anything happened to Herbert? What is it?"

Her husband interposed. "There, there, Mother," he said hastily. "Sit down, and don't jump to conclusions. You've not brought bad news, I'm sure, sir,"

"I'm sorry——," began the visitor.

"Is he hurt?" demanded the mother.

The visitor bowed in assent. "Badly hurt," he said quietly, "but he is not in any pain."

"Oh, thank God!" said the old woman, clasping her hands. "Thank God for that! Thank——"

She broke off suddenly as the sinister meaning of the assurance dawned upon her and she saw the awful confirmation of her fears in the other's averted face. She caught her breath, and turning to her slow-witted husband, laid her trembling old hand upon his. There was a long silence. Each was loath to pursue it further.

"He was caught in the machinery," said the visitor at length, in a low voice.

"Caught in the machinery," repeated Mr. White, in a dazed fashion, "yes."

He sat staring blackly out at the window, and taking his wife's hand between his own, pressed it as he had been wont to do in their old courting days nearly forty years before.

"He was the only one left to us," he said, turning gently to the visitor. "It is hard."

The other coughed, and rising, walked slowly to the window. "The firm wished me to convey their sincere sympathy with you in your great loss," he said, without looking around. "I beg that you will understand I am only their servant and merely obeying orders."

There was no reply; the old woman's face was white, her eyes staring, and her breath inaudible; on the husband's face was a look such as his friend, the sergeant, might have carried into his first action.

"I was to say that Maw and Meggins disclaim all responsibility," continued the other. "They admit no liability at all, but in consideration of your son's services they wish to present you with a certain sum as compensation."

Mr. White dropped his wife's hand, and rising to his feet, gazed with a look of horror at his visitor. His dry lips shaped the words. "How much?"

"Two hundred pounds," was the answer.

Unconscious of his wife's shriek, the old man smiled faintly, put out his hand like a sightless man and dropped, a senseless heap, to the floor.

In the huge new cemetery, some two miles distant, the old people buried their dead son, and came back to a house steeped in shadow and silence.

It was all over so quickly that at first they could hardly realize it, and remained in a state of expectation, as though of something else to happen—something else to happen—something else which was to lighten this load, too heavy for old hearts to bear.

But the days passed, and expectation gave place to resignation—the hopeless resignation of the old, sometimes miscalled apathy. Sometimes they hardly exchanged a word, for now they had nothing to talk about, and their days were long to weariness.

It was about a week after that that the old man, waking suddenly in the night, stretched out his hand and found himself alone. The room was in darkness, and the sound of subdued weeping came from the window. He raised himself in bed and listened.

"Come back," he said tenderly. "You will be cold."

"It is colder for my son," said the old woman, and wept afresh.

The sound of her sobs died away on his ears. The bed was warm, and his eyes heavy with sleep. He dozed fitfully, and then slept, until a sudden wild cry from his wife awoke him with a start.

"The monkey's paw!" she cried wildly. "The monkey's paw!"

He started up in alarm. "Where? Where is it? What's the matter?"

She came stumbling across the room toward him. "I want it," she said quietly. "You've not destroyed it?"

"It's in the parlor, on the bracket," he replied, marvelling, "why?"

She cried and laughed together, and bending over, kissed his cheek.

"I only just thought of it," she said hysterically. "Why didn't I think of it before? Why didn't you think of it?"

"Think of what?" he questioned.

"The other two wishes," she replied rapidly. "We've only had one."

"Was not that enough?" he demanded fiercely.

"No," she cried triumphantly; "we'll have one more. Go down and get it quickly, and wish our boy alive again."

The man sat up in bed and flung the bedclothes from his quaking limbs. "Good God, you are mad!" he cried, aghast.

"Get it," she panted, "get it quickly, and wish—Oh, my boy, my boy!"

Her husband struck a match and lit the candle. "Get back to bed," he said unsteadily. "You don't know what you are saying."

"We had the first wish granted," said the old woman feverishly, "why not the second?"

"A coincidence," stammered the old man.

"Go and get it and wish," cried the old woman, and dragged him toward the door.

He went down in the darkness, and felt his way to the parlor, and then to the mantelpiece. The talisman was in its place, and a horrible fear that the unspoken wish might bring his mutilated son before him, ere he could escape from the room seized upon him, and he caught his breath as he found that he had lost the direction of the door. His brow cold with sweat, he felt his way round the table, and groped along the wall until he found himself in the small passage, with the unwholesome thing in his hand.

Even his wife's face seemed changed as he entered the room. It was white and expectant, and to his fears, seemed to have an unnatural look upon it. He was afraid of her.

"Wish!" she cried, in a strong voice.

"It is foolish and wicked," he faltered.

"Wish!" repeated his wife.

He raised his hand. "I wish my son alive again."

The talisman fell to the floor, and he regarded it shudderingly. Then he sank trembling into a chair as the old woman, with burning eyes, walked to the window and raised the blind.

He sat until he was chilled with the cold, glancing occasionally at the figure of the old woman peering through the window. The candle end, which had burnt below the rim of the china candlestick, was throwing pulsating shadows on the ceiling and walls, until, with a flicker larger than the rest, it expired.

The old man, with an unspeakable sense of relief at the failure of the talisman, crept back to his bed, and a minute or two afterward the old woman came silently and apathetically beside him.

Neither spoke, but both lay silently listening to the ticking of the clock. A stair creaked, and a squeaky mouse scurried noisily through the wall. The darkness was oppressive, and after lying for some time screwing up his courage, the husband took the box of matches, and striking one, went downstairs for a candle.

At the foot of the stairs the match went out, and he paused to strike another, and at the same moment a knock, so quiet and stealthy as to be scarcely audible, sounded on the front door.

The matches fell from his hand. He stood motionless, his breath suspended until the knock was repeated. Then he turned and fled swiftly back to his room, and closed the door behind him. A third knock sounded through the house.

"What's that?" cried the old woman, starting up.

"A rat," said the old man, in shaking tones—"a rat. It passed me on the stairs."

His wife sat up in bed listening. A loud knock resounded through the house.

"It's Herbert! It's Herbert!"

She ran to the door, but her husband was before her, and catching her by the arm, held her tightly.

"What are you going to do?" he whispered hoarsely.

"It's my boy; it's Herbert!" she cried, struggling mechanically. "I forgot it was miles away. What are you holding me for? Let go. I must open the door."

"For God's sake don't let it in," cried the old man, trembling.

"You're afraid of your own son," she cried, struggling. "Let me go. I'm coming, Herbert; I'm coming."

There was another knock, and another. The old

woman, with a sudden wrench, broke free and ran from the room. Her husband followed to the landing, and called after her appealingly as she hurried downstairs. He heard the chain rattle back and the bottom bolt drawn slowly and stiffly from the socket. Then the old woman's voice was heard, strained and panting.

"The bolt," she cried loudly. "Come down. I can't reach it."

But her husband was on his hands and knees, groping wildly on the floor in search of the paw. If he could only find it before the thing outside got in! A perfect fusillade of knocks reverberated through the house, and he heard the scraping of a chair as his wife put it down in the passage against the door. He heard the creaking of the bolt as it came slowly back, and at the same moment he found the monkey's paw, and frantically breathed his third and last wish.

The knocking ceased suddenly, although the echoes of it were still in the house. He heard the chair being drawn back and the door being opened. A cold wind rushed up the staircase, and a long, loud wail of disappointment and misery from his wife gave him courage to run down to her side, and then to the gate beyond. The street lamp flickering opposite shone on a quiet and deserted road.

LORD DUNSANY *(1878-1957)*

. . . was born into an old Irish family, and at his father's death in 1899 succeeded to the family title as the 18th Baron Dunsany (pronounced dun SAY ny).

Beginning in 1908, he wrote numerous novels, stories, poems, and plays, mainly of a fanciful nature; several of the plays were produced by the famous Abbey Theatre in Dublin. Actually, though, writing never played more than a secondary role in Lord Dunsany's life, and he devoted the bulk of his time to sport and soldiering.

Though it is as haunting as his fanciful stories, the grotesque "Two Bottles of Relish" is in no way suggestive of fairyland. All the characters have their two feet planted firmly on the ground. It is, in fact, their very ordinariness that is largely responsible for the impact of this very unconventional detective story.

A vegetarian buys

TWO BOTTLES OF RELISH

—and is revealed as a murderer!

SMITHERS IS my name. I'm what you might call a small man, and in a small way of business. I travel for Numnumo, a relish for meats and savories; the world famous relish I ought to say. It's really quite good, no deleterious acids in it, and does not affect the heart; so it is quite easy to push. I wouldn't have got the job if it weren't. But I hope some day to get something that's harder to push, as of course the harder they are to push, the better the pay. At present I can just make my way, with nothing at all over; but then I live in a very expensive flat. It happened like this, and that brings me to my story. And it isn't the story you'd expect from a small man like me, yet there's nobody else to tell it. Those that know anything of it besides me, are all for hushing it up. They won't speak a word of it.

Well, I was looking for a room to live in in London when first I got my job; it had to be in London, to be central; and I went to a block of buildings, very gloomy they looked, and saw the man that ran them and asked him for what I wanted; flats they called them; just a bedroom and a sort of a cupboard. Well he was show- ing a man 'round at the time who was a gent, in fact more than that, so he didn't take much notice of me, the man that ran all those flats didn't, I mean. So I just ran behind for a bit, seeing all sorts of rooms, and wait- ing till I could be shown my class of thing. We came to a very nice flat, a sitting room, bedroom and bath- room, and a sort of little place that they called a hall. And that's how I came to know Linley. He was the bloke that was being shown 'round.

"Bit expensive," he said.

And the man that ran the flats turned away to the window and picked his teeth. It's funny how much you can show by a simple thing like that. What he meant to say was that he'd hundreds of flats like that, and thousands of people looking for them, and he didn't care who had them or whether they all went on look- ing. There was no mistaking him, somehow. And yet he never said a word, only looked away out of the win- dow and picked his teeth. And I ventured to speak to Mr. Linley then; and I said, "How about it, sir, if I paid half, and shared it? I wouldn't be in the way, and I'm out all day, and whatever you said would go, and really I wouldn't be no more in your way than a cat."

You may be surprised at my doing it; and you'll be much more surprised at him accepting it; at least, you would if you knew me, just a small man in a small way of business; and yet I could see at once that he was taking to me more than he was taking to the man at the window.

"But there's only one bedroom," he said.

"I could make up my bed easy in that little room there," I said.

"The hall," said the man looking 'round from the window, without taking his toothpick out.

"And I'd have the bed out of the way and hid in the cupboard by any hour you like," I said.

He looked thoughtful, and the other man looked out over London; and in the end, do you know, he accepted.

"Friend of yours?" said the flat man.

"Yes," answered Mr. Linley.

It was really very nice of him.

I'll tell you why I did it. Able to afford it? Of course not. But I heard him tell the flat man that he had just come down from Oxford and wanted to live for a few months in London. It turned out he wanted just to be comfortable and do nothing for a bit while he looked things over and chose a job, or probably just as long as he could afford it. Well I said to myself, what's the Oxford manner worth in business, especially a business like mine? Why, simply everything you've got. If I picked up only a quarter of it from this Mr. Linley I'd be able to double my sales, and that would soon mean

I'd be given something a lot harder to push, with perhaps treble the pay. Worth it every time. And you can make a quarter of an education go twice as far again, if you're careful with it. I mean you don't have to quote the whole of the Inferno to show that you've read Milton; half a line may do it.

Well, about that story I have to tell. And you mightn't think that a little man like me could make you shudder. Well, I soon forgot about the Oxford manner when we settled down in our flat. I forgot it in the sheer wonder of the man himself. He had a mind like an acrobat's body, like a bird's body. It didn't want education. You didn't notice whether he was educated or not. Ideas were always leaping up in him, things you'd never have thought of. And not only that, but if any ideas were about, he'd sort of catch them. Time and again I've found him knowing just what I was going to say. Not thought-reading, but what they call intuition. I used to try to learn a bit about chess, just to take my thoughts off Num-numo in the evening, when I'd done with it. But problems I never could do. Yet he'd come along and glance at my problem and say, "You probably move that piece first," and I'd say, "But where?" and he'd say, "Oh, one of those three squares." And I'd say, "But it will be taken on all of them." And the piece a queen all the time, mind you. And he'd say, "Yes, it's doing no good there: you're probably meant to lose it."

And, do you know, he'd be right.

You see he'd been following out what the other man

had been thinking. That's what he'd been doing.

Well one day there was that ghastly murder at Unge. I don't know if you remember it. But Seeger had gone down to live with a girl in a bungalow on the North Downs, and that was the first we had heard of him.

The girl had £200, and he got every penny of it and she utterly disappeared. And Scotland Yard couldn't find her.

Well I'd happened to read that Seeger had bought two bottles of Num-numo; for the Otherthorpe police had found out everything about him, except what he did with the girl; and that of course attracted my attention or I should have never thought again about the case or said a word of it to Linley. Num-numo was always on my mind, as I always spent every day pushing it, and that kept me from forgetting the other thing. And so one day I said to Linley, "I wonder with all that knack you have for seeing through a chess problem, and thinking of one thing and another, that you don't have a go at the Otherthorpe mystery. It's a problem as much as chess," I said.

"There's not the mystery in ten murders that there is in one game of chess," he answered.

"It's beaten Scotland Yard," I said.

"Has it?" he asked.

"Knocked them end-wise," I said.

"It shouldn't have done that," he said. And almost immediately after he said, "What are the facts?"

We were both sitting at supper and I told him the facts, as I had them straight from the papers. She was a

pretty blonde, she was small, she was called Nancy
Elth, she had £200, they lived at the bungalow for five
days. After that he stayed there for another fortnight,
but nobody ever saw her alive again. Seeger said she
had gone to South America, but later said he had never
said South America, but South Africa. None of her
money remained in the bank where she had kept it,
and Seeger was shown to have come by at least £150
just at that time. Then Seeger turned out to be a vegetarian, getting all his food from the greengrocer, and
that made the constable in the village of Unge suspicious of him, for a vegetarian was something new to
the constable. He watched Seeger after that, and it's
well he did, for there was nothing that Scotland Yard
asked him that he couldn't tell them about him, except
of course the one thing. And he told the police at Otherthorpe five or six miles away, and they came and took
a hand at it too.

They were able to say, for one thing, that he never
went outside the bungalow and its tidy garden ever
since she disappeared. You see, the more they watched
him the more suspicious they got, as you naturally do if
you're watching a man; so that very soon they were
watching every move he made, but if it hadn't been
for his being a vegetarian they'd never have started to
suspect him, and there wouldn't have been enough
evidence even for Linley. Not that they found out anything much against him, except that £150 dropping in
from nowhere, and it was Scotland Yard that found
that, not the police of Otherthorpe.

No, what the constable of Unge found out was about the larch trees, and that beat Scotland Yard utterly, and beat Linley up to the very last, and of course it beat me. There were ten larch trees in the bit of a garden, and he'd made some sort of an arrangement with the landlord, Seeger had, before he took the bungalow, by which he could do what he liked with the larch trees. And then from about the time that little Nancy Elth must have died he cut every one of them down. Three times a day he went at it for nearly a week, and when they were all down he cut them all up into logs of no more than two feet long and laid them all in neat heaps. You never saw such work. And what for? To give an excuse for the axe was one theory. But the excuse was bigger than the axe: it took him a fortnight, hard work every day. And he could have killed a little thing like Nancy Elth without an axe, and cut her up, too. Another theory was that he wanted firewood, to make away with the body. But he never used it. He left it all standing there in those neat stacks. It fairly beat everybody.

Well, those are the facts I told Linley. Oh yes, and he bought a big butcher's knife. Funny thing, they all do. And yet it isn't so funny after all; if you've got to cut a woman up, you've got to cut her up; and you can't do that without a knife. Then, there were some negative facts. He hadn't burned her. Only had a fire in the small stove now and then, and only used it for cooking. They got on to that pretty smartly, the Unge constable did, and the men that were lending him a hand from

Otherthorpe. There were some little woody places lying 'round, shaws they call them in that part of the country, the country people do, and they could climb a tree handy and unobserved and get a sniff at the smoke in almost any direction it might be blowing. They did now and then and there was no smell of flesh burning, just ordinary cooking. Pretty smart of the Otherthorpe police that was, though of course it didn't help to hang Seeger. Then later on the Scotland Yard men went down and got another fact, negative but narrowing things down all the while. And that was that the chalk under the bungalow and under the little garden had none of it been disturbed. And he'd never been outside it since Nancy disappeared. Oh yes, and he had a big file besides the knife. But there was no sign of any ground bones found on the file, or any blood on the knife. He'd washed them of course. I told all that to Linley.

Now I ought to warn you before I go any further; I am a small man myself and you probably don't expect anything horrible from me. But I ought to warn you this man was a murderer, or at any rate somebody was; the woman had been made away with, a nice pretty little girl, too, and the man that had done that wasn't necessarily going to stop at things you might think he'd stop at. With the mind to do a thing like that, and with the shadow of the rope to drive him further, you can't say what he'll stop at. Murder tales seem nice things sometimes for a lady to sit and read all by herself by the fire. But murder isn't a nice thing, and when a murderer's desperate and trying to hide his tracks he isn't even as nice as he was before. I'll ask you to bear that in mind. Well, I've warned you.

So I says to Linley, "And what do you make of it?"

"Drains?" said Linley.

"No," I says, "you're wrong there. Scotland Yard has been into that. And the Otherthorpe people before them. They've had a look in the drains, such as they are, a little thing running into a cesspool beyond the garden; and nothing has gone down it, nothing that oughtn't to have, I mean."

He made one or two other suggestions, but Scotland Yard had been before him in every case. That's really the crab of my story, if you'll excuse the expression. You want a man who sets out to be a detective to take his magnifying glass and go down to the spot; to go to the spot before everything; and then to measure the footmarks and pick up the clues and find the knife that the police have overlooked. But Linley never went near the place, and he hadn't got a magnifying glass, not as I ever saw, and Scotland Yard was before him every time.

In fact they had more clues than anybody could make head or tail of. Every kind of clue to show that he'd murdered the poor little girl; every kind of clue to show that he hadn't disposed of the body; and yet the body wasn't there. It wasn't in South America, either, and not much more likely in South Africa. And all the time, mind you, that enormous bunch of chopped larch wood, a clue that was staring everyone in the face and leading nowhere. No we didn't seem to want any more clues, and Linley never went near the place. The trouble was to deal with the clues we'd got. I was completely mystified; so was Scotland Yard; and Linley seemed to be getting no forwarder; and all the while the mystery was hanging on me. I mean if it were not for the trifle I'd chanced to remember, and if it were not for one chance word I said to Linley, that mystery would have gone the way of all the other mysteries that men have made nothing of, a darkness, a little patch of night in history.

Well, the fact was Linley didn't take much interest in it at first, but I was so absolutely sure that he could do it, that I kept him to the idea. "You can do chess problems," I said.

"That's ten times harder," he said, sticking to his point.

"Then why don't you do this?" I said.

"Then go and take a look at the board for me," said Linley.

That was his way of talking. We'd been a fortnight together, and I knew it by now. He meant go down to the bungalow at Unge. I know you'll say why didn't he go himself, but the plain truth of it is that if he'd been tearing about the countryside he'd never have been thinking, whereas sitting there in his chair by the fire in our flat there was no limit to the ground he could cover, if you follow my meaning. So down I went by train next day, and got out at Unge station. And there were the North Downs rising up before me.

"It's up there isn't it?" I said to the porter.

"That's right," he said. "Up there by the lane; and mind to turn to your right when you get to the old yew tree, a very big tree, you can't mistake it, and then . . ." and he told me the way so that I couldn't go wrong. I found them all like that, very nice and helpful. You see it was Unge's day at last; everyone had heard of Unge now; you could have got a letter there any time just then without putting the county or post town; and that was what Unge had to show. I dare say if you tried to find Unge now . . .; well, anyway, they were making hay while the sun shone.

Well, there the hill was, going up into sunlight, going up like a song. You don't want to hear about the spring, and all the May colors that came down over everything later on in the day, and all those birds; but I thought, "What a nice place to bring a girl to." And then when I thought that he'd killed her there, well I'm only a small man, as I said, but when I thought of her on that hill with all the birds singing I said to my-self, "Wouldn't it be odd if it turned out to be me after all that got that man killed, if he did murder her."

So I soon found my way up to the bungalow and began prying about, looking over the hedge into the garden. And I didn't find much, and I found nothing at all that the police hadn't found already, but there were those heaps of larch logs staring me in the face and looking very queer.

I did a lot of thinking, leaning against the hedge, breathing the smell of the May, and looking over the top of it at the larch logs, and the neat little bungalow the other side of the garden. Lots of theories I thought of; till I came to the best thought of all; and that was that if I left the thinking to Linley, with his Oxford-and-Cambridge education, and only brought him the facts, as he had told me, I should be doing more good in my way than if I tried to do any big thinking. I forgot to say that I had gone to Scotland Yard in the morning. Well, there wasn't really much to tell. What they asked me was, what I wanted. And, not having an answer exactly ready, I didn't find out very much from them.

But it was quite different at Unge; everyone was most obliging; it was their day there, as I said. The constable let me go indoors, so long as I didn't touch anything, and he gave me a look at the garden from the inside. And I saw the stumps of the ten larch trees, and I noticed one thing that Linley said was very observant of me, not that it turned out to be any use, but anyway I was doing my best; I noticed that the stumps had been all chopped anyhow. And from that I thought that the man that did it didn't know much about chopping. The constable said this was a deduction. So then I said that the axe was blunt when he used it; and that certainly made the constable think, though he didn't actually say I was right this time.

Did I tell you that Seeger never went outdoors, except to the little garden to chop wood, ever since Nancy disappeared? I think I did. Well it was perfectly true. They'd watched him night and day, one or another of them, and the Unge constable told me that himself. That limited things a good deal. The only thing I didn't like about it was that I felt Linley ought to have found all that out instead of ordinary policemen, and I felt that he could have too. There'd have been romance in a story like that. And they'd never have done it if the news hadn't gone 'round that the man was a vegetarian and only dealt at the greengrocers. Likely as not even that was only started out of pique by the butcher. It's queer what little things may trip a man up. Best to keep straight is my motto. But perhaps I'm straying a bit away from my story. I should like to do that forever; forget that it ever was; but I can't.

Well I picked up all sorts of information; clues I suppose I should call it in a story like this; though they none of them seemed to lead anywhere. For instance, I found out everything he ever bought at the village; I could even tell you the kind of salt he bought, quite plain with no phosphates in it, that they sometimes put in to make it tidy. And then he got ice from the fishmongers, and plenty of vegetables, as I said, from the greengrocer, Mergin and Sons. And I had a bit of talk over it all with the constable. Slugger he said his name was. I wondered why he hadn't come in and searched the place as soon as the girl was missing. "Well, you can't do that," he said. "And besides, we didn't suspect at once, not about the girl, that is. We only suspected there was something wrong about him on account of him being a vegetarian. He stayed a good fortnight after the last was seen of her. And then we slipped in like a knife. But, you see, no one had been inquiring about her, there was no warrant out."

"And what did you find," I asked Slugger, "when you went in?"

"Just a big file," he said, "and the knife and the axe that he must have got to chop her up with."

"But he got the axe to chop trees with," I said.

"Well, yes," he said, but rather grudgingly.

"And what did he chop them for?" I asked.

"Well of course my superiors have theories about that," he said, "that they mightn't tell to everybody."

You see, it was those logs that were beating them.

"But did he cut her up at all?" I asked.

"Well, he said that she was going to South America," he answered. Which was really very fair-minded of him.

I don't remember now much else that he told me. Seeger left the plates and dishes all washed up and very neat, he said.

Well, I brought all this back to Linley, going up by the train that started just about sunset. I'd like to tell you about the late spring evening, so calm over that grim bungalow; but you'll want to hear of the murder. Well, I told Linley everything, though much of it didn't seem to me to be worth the telling. The trouble was that the moment I began to leave anything out, he'd know it, and make me drag it in. "You can't tell what mày be vital," he'd say. "A tin tack swept away by a housemaid might hang a man," he'd say.

All very well, but be consistent even if you are educated at Eton and Harrow; and whenever I mentioned Num-numo, which after all was the beginning of the whole story, because he wouldn't have heard of it if it hadn't been for me, and my noticing that Seeger had bought two bottles of it, why then he said that things like that were trivial and we should keep to the main issues. I naturally talked a bit about Num-numo, because only that day I had pushed close on fifty bottles of it in Unge. A murder certainly stimulates people's minds, and Seeger's two bottles gave me an opportunity that only a fool could have failed to make something of. But of course all that was nothing at all to Linley.

You can't see a man's thoughts and you can't look into his mind, so that all the most exciting things in the world can never be told of. But what I think happened all that evening with Linley, while I talked to him before supper, and all through supper, and sitting smoking afterwards in front of our fire, was that his thoughts were stuck at a barrier there was no getting over. And the barrier wasn't the difficulty of finding ways and means by which Seeger might have made away with the body, but the impossibility of finding why he chopped those masses of wood every day for a fortnight, and paid as I'd just found out, £25 to his landlord to be allowed to do it. That's what was beating Linley. As for the ways by which Seeger might have hidden the body, it seemed to me that every way was blocked by the police. If you said he buried it they said the chalk was undisturbed, if you said he carried

it away they said he never left the place, if you said he
burned it they said no smell of burning was ever
noticed when the smoke blew low, and when it didn't
they climbed trees after it. I'd taken to Linley wonderfully, and I didn't have to be educated to see there was
something big in a mind like his, and I thought that he
could have done it. When I saw the police getting in
before him like that, and no way that I could see of
getting past them, I felt real sorry.

Did anyone come to the house, he asked me once or
twice? Did anyone take anything away from it? But we
couldn't account for it that way. Then perhaps I made
some suggestion that was no good, or perhaps I started
talking of Num-numo again, and he interrupted me
rather sharply.

"But what would you do, Smithers?" he said. "What
would you do yourself?"

"If I'd murdered poor Nancy Elth?" I asked.

"Yes," he said.

"I can't ever imagine doing such a thing," I told him.

He sighed at that, as though it were something
against me.

"I suppose I should never be a detective," I said.
And he just shook his head.

Then he looked broodingly into the fire for what
seemed an hour. And then he shook his head again.
We both went to bed after that.

I shall remember the next day all my life. I was till
evening, as usual, pushing Num-numo. And we sat
down to supper about nine. You couldn't get things

cooked at those flats, so of course we had it cold. And Linley began with a salad. I can see it now, every bit of it. Well, I was still a bit full of what I'd done in Unge, pushing Num-numo. Only a fool, I know, would have been unable to push it there; but still, I *had* pushed it; and about fifty bottles, forty-eight to be exact, are something in a small village, whatever the circumstances. So I was talking about it a bit; and then all of a sudden I realized that Num-numo was nothing to Linley, and I pulled myself up with a jerk. It was really very kind of him; do you know what he did? He must have known at once why I stopped talking, and he just stretched out a hand and said: "Would you give me a little of your Num-numo for my salad?"

I was so touched I nearly gave it him. But of course you don't take Num-numo with salad. Only for meats and savories. That's on the bottle.

So I just said to him, "Only for meats and savories." Though I don't know what savories are. Never had any.

I never saw a man's face go like that before.

He seemed still for a whole minute. And nothing speaking about him but that expression. Like a man that's seen a ghost, one is tempted to say. But it wasn't really at all. I'll tell you what he looked like. Like a man that's seen something that no one has ever looked at before, something he thought couldn't be.

And then he said in a voice that was all quite changed, more low and gentle and quiet it seemed, "No good for vegetables, eh?"

"Not a bit," I said.

And at that he gave a kind of sob in his throat. I hadn't thought he could feel things like that. Of course I didn't know what it was all about; but, whatever it was, I thought all that sort of thing would have been knocked out of him at Eton and Harrow, an educated man like that. There were no tears in his eyes but he was feeling something horribly.

And then he began to speak with big spaces between his words, saying, "A man might make a mistake perhaps, and use Num-numo with vegetables."

"Not twice," I said. What else could I say?

And he repeated that after me as though I had told of the end of the world, and adding an awful emphasis to my words, till they seemed all clammy with some frightful significance, and shaking his head as he said it.

Then he was quite silent.

"What is it?" I asked.

"Smithers," he said.

And I said, "Well?"

"Look here Smithers," he said, "you must phone down to the grocer at Unge and find out from him this."

"Yes?"

"Whether Seeger bought those two bottles, as I expect he did, on the same day, and not a few days apart. He couldn't have done that."

I waited to see if any more was coming, and then I ran out and did what I was told. It took me some time, being after nine o'clock, and only then with the help of the police. About six days apart they said; and so I came back and told Linley. He looked up at me so hopefully when I came in, but I saw that it was the wrong answer by his eyes.

You can't take things to heart like that without being ill, and when he didn't speak I said, "What you want is a good brandy, and go to bed early."

And he said, "No. I must see someone from Scotland Yard. Phone 'round to them. Say here at once."

But I said, "I can't get an inspector from Scotland Yard to call on us at this hour."

His eyes were all lit up. He was all there all right.

"Then tell them," he said, "they'll never find Nancy Elth. Tell one of them to come here and I'll tell him why." And he added, I think only for me, "They must watch Seeger, till one day they get him over something else."

And, do you know, he came. Inspector Ulton; he came himself.

While we were waiting I tried to talk to Linley. Partly curiosity, I admit. But I didn't want to leave him to those thoughts of his, brooding away by the fire. I tried to ask him what it was all about. But he wouldn't tell me. "Murder is horrible," is all he would say. "And as a man covers his tracks up it only gets worse."

He wouldn't tell me. "There are tales," he said, "that one never wants to hear."

That's true enough. I wish I'd never heard this one. I never did actually. But I guessed it from Linley's last words to Inspector Ulton, the only ones that I over-heard. And perhaps this is the point at which to stop reading my story, so that you don't guess it too; even if you think you want murder stories. For don't you rather want a murder story with a bit of romantic twist, and not a story about real foul murder? Well, just as you like.

In came Inspector Ulton, and Linley shook hands in silence, and pointed the way to his bedroom; and they went in there and talked in low voices, and I never heard a word.

A fairly hearty-looking man was the inspector when they went into that room.

They walked through our sitting room in silence when they came out, and together they went into the hall, and there I heard the only words they said to each other. It was the inspector that first broke that silence.

"But why," he said, "did he cut down the trees?"

"Solely," said Linley, "in order to get an appetite."

EDGAR ALLAN POE *(1809-1849)*

. . . was orphaned at the age of two and, though never legally adopted, was given a home by a rich Scottish merchant, John Allan, whose name he combined with his own.

While still a student at the University of Virginia, Poe got into trouble because of his gambling and drinking; from then on he tormented himself with drink and with his ever-present fear of insanity.

Described by George Bernard Shaw as "This finest of finest of artists," Poe has been celebrated for over a century as one of the truly great American writers and poets. "The Cask of Amontillado" is an extraordinarily compelling portrayal of a madman, the maniacal Montresor who would go to any length to defend his family motto: Nemo me impune lacessit *(No one attacks me with impunity). This tale is considered a classic among horror stories—and, indeed, among short stories of any genre.*

Two men go down to taste

THE CASK OF AMONTILLADO

but only one comes back!

THE THOUSAND INJURIES of Fortunato I had borne as I best could; but when he ventured upon insult, I vowed revenge. You, who so well know the nature of my soul, will not suppose, however, that I gave utterance to a threat. *At length* I would be avenged; this was a point definitively settled—but the very definitiveness with which it was resolved, precluded the idea of risk. I must not only punish, but punish with impunity. A wrong is unredressed when retribution overtakes its redresser. It is equally unredressed when the avenger fails to make himself felt as such to him who has done the wrong.

It must be understood, that neither by word nor deed had I given Fortunato cause to doubt my good-will. I continued, as was my wont, to smile in his face, and he did not perceive that my smile *now* was at the thought of his immolation.

He had a weak point—this Fortunato—although in other regards he was a man to be respected and even feared. He prided himself on his connoisseurship in wine. Few Italians have the true virtuoso spirit. For the most part their enthusiasm is adopted to suit the time and opportunity—to practice imposture upon the British and Austrian *millionnaires.* In painting and gemmary Fortunato, like his countrymen, was a quack—but in the matter of old wines he was sincere. In this respect I did not differ from him materially: I was skillful in the Italian vintages myself, and bought largely whenever I could.

It was about dusk, one evening during the supreme madness of the carnival season, that I encountered my friend. He accosted me with excessive warmth, for he had been drinking much. The man wore motley. He had on a tight-fitting parti-striped dress, and his head was surmounted by the conical cap and bells. I was so pleased to see him, that I thought I should never have done wringing his hand.

I said to him: "My dear Fortunato, you are luckily met. How remarkably well you are looking to-day! But I have received a pipe of what passes for Amontillado, and I have my doubts."

"How?" said he. "Amontillado? A pipe? Impossible! And in the middle of the carnival!"

"I have my doubts," I replied; "and I was silly enough to pay the full Amontillado price without consulting you in the matter. You were not to be found, and I was fearful of losing a bargain."

"Amontillado!"

"I have my doubts."

"Amontillado!"

"And I must satisfy them."

"Amontillado!"

"As you are engaged, I am on my way to Luchesi. If any one has a critical turn, it is he. He will tell me——"

"Luchesi cannot tell Amontillado from Sherry."

"And yet some fools will have it that his taste is a match for your own."

"Come, let us go."

"Whither?"

"To your vaults."

"My friend, no; I will not impose upon your good nature. I perceive you have an engagement. Luchesi——"

"I have no engagement;—come."

"My friend, no. It is not the engagement, but the severe cold with which I perceive you are afflicted. The vaults are insufferably damp. They are encrusted with nitre."

"Let us go, nevertheless. The cold is merely nothing. Amontillado! You have been imposed upon. And as for Luchesi, he cannot distinguish Sherry from Amontillado."

Thus speaking, Fortunato possessed himself of my arm. Putting on a mask of black silk, and drawing a *roquelaire* closely about my person, I suffered him to hurry me to my palazzo.

There were no attendants at home; they had absconded to make merry in honor of the time. I had told them that I should not return until the morning, and had given them explicit orders not to stir from the house. These orders were sufficient, I well knew, to insure their immediate disappearance, one and all, as soon as my back was turned.

I took from their sconces two flambeaux, and giving one to Fortunato, bowed him through several suites of rooms to the archway that led into the vaults. I passed down a long and winding staircase, requesting him to be cautious as he followed. We came at length to the foot of the descent, and stood together on the damp ground of the catacombs of the Montresors.

The gait of my friend was unsteady, and the bells upon his cap jingled as he strode.

"The pipe?" said he.

"It is farther on," said I; "but observe the white webwork which gleams from these cavern walls."

He turned toward me, and looked into my eyes with two filmy orbs that distilled the rheum of intoxication.

"Nitre?" he asked, at length.

"Nitre," I replied. "How long have you had that cough?"

"Ugh! ugh! ugh!—ugh! ugh! ugh!—ugh! ugh! ugh! —ugh! ugh! ugh!—ugh! ugh! ugh!"

My poor friend found it impossible to reply for many minutes.

"It is nothing," he said, at last.

"Come," I said, with decision, "we will go back; your

health is precious. You are rich, respected, admired, be-loved; you are happy, as once I was. You are a man to be missed. For me it is no matter. We will go back; you will be ill, and I cannot be responsible. Besides, there is Luchesi——"

"Enough," he said; "the cough is a mere nothing; it will not kill me. I shall not die of a cough."

"True—true," I replied; "and, indeed, I had no inten-tion of alarming you unnecessarily; but you should use all proper caution. A draught of this Medoc will defend us from the damps."

Here I knocked off the neck of a bottle which I drew from a long row of its fellows that lay upon the mould.

"Drink," I said, presenting him the wine.

He raised it to his lips with a leer. He paused and nodded to me familiarly, while his bells jingled.

"I drink," he said, "to the buried that repose around us."

"And I to your long life."

He again took my arm, and we proceeded.

"These vaults," he said, "are extensive."

"The Montresors," I replied, "were a great and nu-merous family."

"I forget your arms."

"A huge human foot d'or, in a field azure; the foot crushes a serpent rampant whose fangs are imbedded in the heel."

"And the motto?"

"Nemo me impune lacessit."

"Good!" he said.

The wine sparkled in his eyes and the bells jingled. My own fancy grew warm with the Medoc. We had passed through walls of piled bones, with casks and puncheons intermingling, into the inmost recesses of the catacombs. I paused again, and this time I made bold to seize Fortunato by an arm above the elbow.

"The nitre!" I said; "see, it increases. It hangs like moss upon the vaults. We are below the river's bed. The drops of moisture trickle among the bones. Come, we will go back ere it is too late. Your cough——"

"It is nothing," he said; "let us go on. But first, another draught of the Medoc."

I broke and reached him a flagon of De Grâve. He emptied it at a breath. His eyes flashed with a fierce light. He laughed and threw the bottle upward with a gesticulation I did not understand.

I looked at him in surprise. He repeated the movement—a grotesque one.

"You do not comprehend?" he said.

"Not I," I replied.

"Then you are not of the brotherhood."

"How?"

"You are not of the Masons."

"Yes, yes," I said; "yes, yes."

"You? Impossible! A Mason?"

"A mason," I replied.

"A sign," he said.

"It is this," I answered, producing a trowel from beneath the folds of my *roquelaire*.

"You jest," he exclaimed, recoiling a few paces. "But

let us proceed to the Amontillado."

"Be it so," I said, replacing the tool beneath the cloak, and again offering him my arm. He leaned upon it heavily. We continued our route in search of the Amontillado. We passed through a range of low arches, descended, passed on, and descending again, arrived at a deep crypt, in which the foulness of the air caused our flambeaux rather to glow than flame.

At the most remote end of the crypt there appeared another less spacious. Its walls had been lined with human remains, piled to the vault overhead, in the fashion of the great catacombs of Paris. Three sides of this interior crypt were still ornamented in this manner. From the fourth the bones had been thrown down, and lay promiscuously upon the earth, forming at one point a mound of some size. Within the wall thus exposed by the displacing of the bones, we perceived a still interior recess, in depth about four feet, in width three, in height six or seven. It seemed to have been constructed for no especial use within itself, but formed merely the interval between two of the colossal supports of the roof of the catacombs, and was backed by one of their circumscribing walls of solid granite.

It was in vain that Fortunato, uplifting his dull torch, endeavored to pry into the depth of the recess. Its termination the feeble light did not enable us to see.

"Proceed," I said; "herein is the Amontillado. As for Luchesi——"

"He is an ignoramus," interrupted my friend, as he stepped unsteadily forward, while I followed immediately at his heels. In an instant he had reached the extremity of the niche, and finding his progress arrested by the rock, stood stupidly bewildered. A moment more and I had fettered him to the granite. In its surface were two iron staples, distant from each other about two feet, horizontally. From one of these depended a short chain, from the other a padlock. Throwing the links about his waist, it was but the work of a few seconds to secure it. He was too much astounded to resist. Withdrawing the key I stepped back from the recess.

"Pass your hand," I said, "over the wall; you cannot help feeling the nitre. Indeed it is *very* damp. Once more let me *implore* you to return. No? Then I must positively leave you. But I must first render you all the little attentions in my power."

"The Amontillado!" ejaculated my friend, not yet recovered from his astonishment.

"True," I replied, "the Amontillado."

As I said these words I busied myself among the pile of bones of which I have before spoken. Throwing them aside, I soon uncovered a quantity of building stone and mortar. With these materials and with the aid of my trowel, I began vigorously to wall up the entrance of the niche.

I had scarcely laid the first tier of the masonry when I discovered that the intoxication of Fortunato had in a great measure worn off. The earliest indication I had of this was a low moaning cry from the depth of the recess. It was *not* the cry of a drunken man. There was then a long and obstinate silence. I laid the second tier, and the third, and the fourth; and then I heard the furious vibrations of the chain. The noise lasted for several minutes, during which, that I might hearken to it with the more satisfaction, I ceased my labors and sat down upon the bones. When at last the clanking subsided, I resumed the trowel, and finished without interruption the fifth, the sixth, and the seventh tier. The wall was now nearly upon a level with my breast. I again paused, and holding the flambeaux over the mason-work, threw a few feeble rays upon the figure within.

A succession of loud and shrill screams, bursting suddenly from the throat of the chained form, seemed to thrust me violently back. For a brief moment I hesitated —I trembled. Unsheathing my rapier, I began to grope with it about the recess; but the thought of an instant reassured me. I placed my hand upon the solid fabric of the catacombs, and felt satisfied. I reapproached the wall. I replied to the yells of him who clamored. I re-echoed —I aided—I surpassed them in volume and in strength. I did this, and the clamorer grew still.

It was now midnight, and my task was drawing to a close. I had completed the eighth, the ninth, and the tenth tier. I had finished a portion of the last and the eleventh; there remained but a single stone to be fitted and plastered in. I struggled with its weight; I placed it partially in its destined position. But now there came from out the niche a low laugh that erected the hairs upon my head. It was succeeded by a sad voice, which I had difficulty in recognizing as that of the noble Fortunato. The voice said—

"Ha! ha! ha!—he! he!—a very good joke indeed—an excellent jest. We will have many a rich laugh about it at the palazzo—he! he! he!—over our wine—he! he! he!"

"The Amontillado!" I said.

"He! he! he!—he! he! he!—yes, the Amontillado. But is it not getting late? Will not they be awaiting us at the palazzo, the Lady Fortunato and the rest? Let us be gone."

"Yes," I said, "let us be gone."

"For the love of God, Montresor!"

"Yes," I said, "for the love of God!"

But to these words I hearkened in vain for a reply. I grew impatient. I called aloud:

"Fortunato!"

No answer. I called again:

"Fortunato!"

No answer still. I thrust a torch through the remaining aperture and let it fall within. There came forth in return only a jingling of the bells. My heart grew sick—on account of the dampness of the catacombs. I hastened to make an end of my labor. I forced the last stone into its position; I plastered it up. Against the new masonry I re-erected the old rampart of bones. For the half of a century no mortal has disturbed them. *In pace requiescat!*

Even the most brutal madman

could not have committed

THE MURDERS
IN THE RUE MORGUE

AS THE STRONG MAN exults in his physical ability, delighting in such exercises as call his muscles into action, so glories the analyst in that moral activity which *disentangles*. He derives pleasure from even the most trivial occupations bringing his talent into play.

The narrative which follows will appear to the reader somewhat in the light of a commentary upon the proposition just advanced.

Residing in Paris during the spring and part of the summer of 18—, I there became acquainted with a Monsieur C. Auguste Dupin.

Our first meeting was at an obscure library in the Rue Montmartre, where the accident of our both being in search of the same very rare and very remarkable volume brought us into closer communion. We saw each other again and again. I was deeply interested in the little family history which he detailed to me with all that candor which a Frenchman indulges whenever mere self is the theme. I was astonished, too, at the vast extent of his reading; and, above all, I felt my soul enkindled within me by the wild fervor, and the vivid freshness of his imagination. Seeking in Paris the objects I then sought, I felt that the society of such a man would be to me a treasure beyond price; and this feeling I frankly confided to him. It was at length arranged that we should live together during my stay in the city; and as my worldly circumstances were somewhat less embarrassed than his own, I was permitted to be at the expense of renting, and furnishing in a style which suited the rather fantastic gloom of our common temper, a time-eaten and grotesque mansion, long deserted through superstitions into which we did not inquire, and tottering to its fall in a retired and desolate portion of the Faubourg St. Germain.

Not long after this, we were looking over an evening edition of the *Gazette des Tribunaux,* when the following paragraphs arrested our attention.

"EXTRAORDINARY MURDERS. — This morning, about three o'clock, the inhabitants of the Quartier St. Roch were roused from sleep by a succession of terrific shrieks, issuing, apparently, from the fourth story of a house in the Rue Morgue, known to be in the sole occupancy of one Madame L'Espanaye, and her daughter, Mademoiselle Camille L'Espanaye. After

some delay, occasioned by a fruitless attempt to procure admission in the usual manner, the gateway was
broken in with a crowbar, and eight or ten of the neighbors entered, accompanied by two *gendarmes.* By this
time the cries had ceased; but, as the party rushed up
the first flight of stairs, two or more rough voices, in
angry contention, were distinguished, and seemed to
proceed from the upper part of the house. As the second landing was reached, these sounds, also, had
ceased, and everything remained perfectly quiet. The
party spread themselves, and hurried from room to
room. Upon arriving at a large back chamber in the
fourth story (the door of which, being found locked,
with the key inside, was forced open), a spectacle pre-
sented itself which struck every one present not less
with horror than with astonishment.

"The apartment was in the wildest disorder—the
furniture broken and thrown about in all directions.
There was only one bedstead; and from this the bed
had been removed, and thrown into the middle of the
floor. On a chair lay a razor, besmeared with blood.
On the hearth were two or three long and thick tresses
of gray human hair, also dabbled with blood, and
seeming to have been pulled out by the roots. Upon
the floor were found four Napoleons, an ear-ring of
topaz, three large silver spoons, three smaller of
métal d'Alger, and two bags, containing nearly four
thousand francs in gold. The drawers of a *bureau,*
which stood in one corner, were open, and had been,
apparently, rifled, although many articles still re-

mained in them. A small iron safe was discovered under the *bed* (not under the bedstead). It was open, with the key still in the door. It had no contents beyond a few old letters, and other papers of little consequence.

"Of Madame L'Espanaye no traces were here seen; but an unusual quantity of soot being observed in the fireplace, a search was made in the chimney, and (horrible to relate!) the corpse of the daughter, head downward, was dragged therefrom; it having been thus forced up the narrow aperture for a considerable distance. The body was quite warm. Upon examining it, many excoriations were perceived, no doubt occasioned by the violence with which it had been thrust up and disengaged. Upon the face were many severe scratches, and, upon the throat, dark bruises, and deep indentations of finger nails, as if the deceased had been throttled to death.

"After a thorough investigation of every portion of the house without farther discovery, the party made its way into a small paved yard in the rear of the building, where lay the corpse of the old lady, with her throat so entirely cut that, upon an attempt to raise her, the head fell off. The body, as well as the head, was fearfully mutilated—the former so much so as scarcely to retain any semblance of humanity.

"To this horrible mystery there is not as yet, we believe, the slightest clew."

The next day's paper had these additional particulars:

"The Tragedy in the Rue Morgue.—Many individuals

have been examined in relation to this most extraordinary and frightful affair," [the word *'affaire'* has not yet, in France, that levity of import which it conveys with us] "but nothing whatever has transpired to throw light upon it. We give below all the material testimony elicited.

"*Pauline Dubourg,* laundress, deposes that she has known both the deceased for three years, having washed for them during that period. The old lady and her daughter seemed on good terms—very affectionate toward each other. They were excellent pay. Could not speak in regard to their mode or means of living. Believe that Madame L. told fortunes for a living. Was reputed to have money put by. Never met any person in the house when she called for the clothes or took them home. Was sure that they had no servant in employ. There appeared to be no furniture in any part of the building except in the fourth story.

"*Pierre Moreau,* tobacconist, deposes that he has been in the habit of selling small quantities of tobacco and snuff to Madame L'Espanaye for nearly four years. Was born in the neighborhood, and has always resided there. The deceased and her daughter had occupied the house in which the corpses were found, for more than six years. It was formerly occupied by a jeweller, who underlet the upper rooms to various persons. The house was the property of Madame L. She became dissatisfied with the abuse of the premises by her tenant, and moved into them herself, refusing to let any portion. The old lady was childish. Witness had seen the daughter some five or six times during the six years. The two lived an exceedingly retired life—were reputed to have money. Had heard it said among the neighbors that Madame L. told fortunes—did not believe it. Had never seen any person enter the door except the old lady and her daughter, a porter once or twice, and a physician some eight or ten times.

"Many other persons, neighbors, gave evidence to the same effect. No one was spoken of as frequenting the house. It was not known whether there were any living connections of Madame L. and her daughter. The shutters of the front windows were seldom opened. Those in the rear were always closed, with the exception of the large back room, fourth story. The house was a good house—not very old.

"*Isidore Musèt, gendarme,* deposes that he was called to the house about three o'clock in the morning, and found some twenty or thirty persons at the gateway, endeavoring to gain admittance. Forced it open, at length, with a bayonet—not with a crowbar. Had but little difficulty in getting it open, on account of its being a double or folding gate, and bolted neither at bottom nor top. The shrieks were continued until the gate was forced—and then suddenly ceased. They seemed to be screams of some person (or persons) in great agony—were loud and drawn out, not short and quick. Witness led the way up stairs. Upon reaching the first landing, heard two voices in loud and angry contention—the one a gruff voice, the other much shriller—a very strange voice. Could distinguish some words of the former, which was

that of a Frenchman. Was positive that it was not a
woman's voice. Could distinguish the words *'sacré'* and
'diable.' The shrill voice was that of a foreigner. Could
not be sure whether it was the voice of a man or of a
woman. Could not make out what was said, but believed
the language to be Spanish. The state of the room and of
the bodies was described by this witness as we described
them yesterday.

"*Henri Duval,* a neighbor, and by trade a silver-
smith, deposes that he was one of the party who first
entered the house. Corroborates the testimony of Musèt
in general. As soon as they forced an entrance, they reclosed the door, to keep out the crowd, which collected
very fast, notwithstanding the lateness of the hour. The
shrill voice, this witness thinks, was that of an Italian.
Was certain it was not French. Could not be sure that it
was a man's voice. It might have been a woman's. Was
not acquainted with the Italian language. Could not distinguish the words, but was convinced by the intonation
that the speaker was an Italian. Knew Madame L. and
her daughter. Had conversed with both frequently. Was
sure that the shrill voice was not that of either of the
deceased.

"—— *Odenheimer, restaurateur.*—This witness volun-
teered his testimony. Not speaking French, was examined through an interpreter. Is a native of Amsterdam.
Was passing the house at the time of the shrieks. They
lasted for several minutes—probably ten. They were
long and loud—very awful and distressing. Was one of
those who entered the building. Corroborated the pre-

vious evidence in every respect but one. Was sure that the shrill voice was that of a man—of a Frenchman. Could not distinguish the words uttered. They were loud and quick—unequal—spoken apparently in fear as well as in anger. The voice was harsh—not so much shrill as harsh. Could not call it a shrill voice. The gruff voice said repeatedly, *'sacré,' 'diable,'* and once *'mon Dieu.'*

'Jules Mignaud, banker, of the firm of Mignaud et Fils, Rue Deloraine. Is the elder Mignaud. Madame L'Espanaye had some property. Had opened an account with his banking house in the spring of the year—— (eight years previously). Made frequent deposits in small sums. Had checked for nothing until the third day before her death, when she took out in person the sum of 4000 francs. This sum was paid in gold, and a clerk sent home with the money.

"Adolphe Le Bon, clerk to Mignaud et Fils, deposes that on the day in question, about noon, he accompanied Madame L'Espanaye to her residence with the 4000 francs, put up in two bags. Upon the door being opened, Mademoiselle L. appeared and took from his hands one of the bags, while the old lady relieved him of the other. He then bowed and departed. Did not see any person in the street at the time. It is a by-street—very lonely.

"William Bird, tailor, deposes that he was one of the party who entered the house. Is an Englishman. Has lived in Paris two years. Was one of the first to ascend the stairs. Heard the voices in contention. The gruff voice was that of a Frenchman. Could make out several words, but cannot now remember all. Heard distinctly

'*sacré*' and '*mon Dieu.*' There was a sound at the moment as if of several persons struggling—a scraping and scuffling sound. The shrill voice was very loud—louder than the gruff one. Is sure that it was not the voice of an Englishman. Appeared to be that of a German. Might have been a woman's voice. Does not understand German.

"Four of the above-named witnesses, being recalled, deposed that the door of the chamber in which was found the body of Mademoiselle L. was locked on the inside when the party reached it. Every thing was perfectly silent—no groans or noises of any kind. Upon forcing the door no person was seen. The windows, both of the back and front room, were down and firmly fastened from within. A door between the two rooms was closed but not locked. The door leading from the front room into the passage was locked, with the key on the inside. A small room in the front of the house, on the fourth story, at the head of the passage, was open, the door being ajar. This room was crowded with old beds, boxes, and so forth. These were carefully removed and searched. There was not an inch of any portion of the house which was not carefully searched. Sweeps were sent up and down the chimneys. The house was a four-story one, with garrets (*mansardes*). A trap-door on the roof was nailed down very securely—did not appear to have been opened for years. The time elapsing between the hearing of the voices in contention and the breaking open of the room door was variously stated by the witnesses. Some made it as short as three minutes—some as long as five.

The door was opened with difficulty.

"*Alfonzo Garcio,* undertaker, deposes that he resides in the Rue Morgue. Is a native of Spain. Was one of the party who entered the house. Did not proceed up stairs. Is nervous, and was apprehensive of the consequences of agitation. Heard the voices in contention. The gruff voice was that of a Frenchman. Could not distinguish what was said. The shrill voice was that of an Englishman—is sure of this. Does not understand the English language, but judges by the intonation.

"*Alberto Montani,* confectioner, deposes that he was among the first to ascend the stairs. Heard the voices in question. The gruff voice was that of a Frenchman. Distinguished several words. The speaker appeared to be expostulating. Could not make out the words of the shrill voice. Spoke quick and unevenly. Thinks it the voice of a Russian. Corroborates the general testimony. Is an Italian. Never conversed with a native of Russia.

"Several witnesses, recalled, here testified that the chimneys of all the rooms on the fourth story were too narrow to admit the passage of a human being. By 'sweeps' were meant cylindrical sweeping-brushes, such as are employed by those who clean chimneys. These brushes were passed up and down every flue in the house. There is no back passage by which any one could have descended while the party proceeded up stairs. The body of Mademoiselle L'Espanaye was so firmly wedged in the chimney that it could not be got down until four or five of the party united their strength.

"*Paul Dumas,* physician, deposes that he was called

to view the bodies about daybreak. They were both then lying on the sacking of the bedstead in the chamber where Mademoiselle L. was found. The corpse of the young lady was much bruised and excoriated. The fact that it had been thrust up the chimney would sufficiently account for these appearances. The throat was greatly chafed. There were several deep scratches just below the chin, together with a series of livid spots which were evidently the impression of fingers. The face was fearfully discolored, and the eyeballs protruded. The tongue had been partially bitten through. A large bruise was discovered upon the pit of the stomach, produced, apparently, by the pressure of a knee. In the opinion of M. Dumas, Mademoiselle L'Espanaye had been throttled to death by some person or persons unknown. The corpse of the mother was horribly mutilated. All the bones of the right leg and arm were more or less shattered. The left *tibia* much splintered, as well as all the ribs of the left side. Whole body dreadfully bruised and discolored. It was not possible to say how the injuries had been inflicted. A heavy club of wood, or a broad bar of iron—a chair—any large, heavy, and obtuse weapon would have produced such results, if wielded by the hands of a very powerful man. No woman could have inflicted the blows with any weapon. The head of the deceased, when seen by witness, was entirely separated from the body, and was also greatly shattered. The throat had evidently been cut with some very sharp instrument—probably with a razor.

"*Alexandre Etienne,* surgeon, was called with M.

Dumas to view the bodies. Corroborated the testimony, and the opinions of M. Dumas.

"Nothing further of importance was elicited, although several other persons were examined. A murder so mysterious, and so perplexing in all its particulars, was never before committed in Paris—if indeed a murder has been committed at all. The police are entirely at fault—an unusual occurrence in affairs of this nature. There is not, however, the shadow of a clew apparent."

The evening edition of the paper stated that the greatest excitement still continued in the Quartier St. Roch—that the premises in question had been carefully re-searched, and fresh examinations of witnesses instituted, but all to no purpose. A postscript, however, mentioned that Adolphe Le Bon had been arrested and imprisoned—although nothing appeared to criminate him beyond the facts already detailed.

Dupin seemed singularly interested in the progress of this affair—at least so I judged from his manner, for he made no comments. It was only after the announcement that Le Bon had been imprisoned, that he asked me my opinion respecting the murders.

I could merely agree with all Paris in considering them an insoluble mystery. I saw no means by which it would be possible to trace the murderer.

"We must not judge of the means," said Dupin, "by this shell of an examination. The Parisian police, so much extolled for *acumen,* are cunning, but no more. There is no method in their proceedings, beyond the method of the moment.

"As for these murders, let us enter into some examinations for ourselves, before we make up an opinion respecting them. An inquiry will afford us amusement," [I thought this an odd term, so applied, but said nothing] "and besides, Le Bon once rendered me a service for which I am not ungrateful. We will go and see the premises with our own eyes. I know G——, the Prefect of Police, and shall have no difficulty in obtaining the necessary permission."

The permission was obtained, and we proceeded at once to the Rue Morgue. This is one of those miserable thoroughfares which intervene between the Rue Richelieu and the Rue St. Roch. It was late in the afternoon when we reached it, as this quarter is at a great distance from that in which we resided. The house was readily found; for there were still many persons gazing up at the closed shutters, with an objectless curiosity, from the opposite side of the way. It was an ordinary Parisian house, with a gateway, on one side of which was a glazed watch-box, with a sliding panel in the window, indicating a *loge de concierge*. Before going in we walked up the street, turned down an alley, and then, again turning, passed in the rear of the building—Dupin, meanwhile, examining the whole neighborhood, as well as the house, with a minuteness of attention for which I could see no possible object.

Retracing our steps we came again to the front of the dwelling, rang, and, having shown our credentials, were admitted by the agents in charge. We went up stairs—into the chamber where the body of Mademoiselle L'Espanaye had been found, and where both the deceased still lay. The disorders of the room had, as usual, been suffered to exist. I saw nothing beyond what had been stated in the *Gazette des Tribunaux*. Dupin scrutinized every thing—not excepting the bodies of the victims. We then went into the other rooms, and into the yard; a *gendarme* accompanying us throughout. The examination occupied us until dark, when we took our departure. On our way home my companion stepped in for a moment at the office of one of the daily papers.

I have said that the whims of my friend were manifold, and that *Je les ménageais:*—for this phrase there is no English equivalent. It was his humor, now, to decline all conversation on the subject of the murder, until about noon the next day. He then asked me, suddenly, if I had observed any thing *peculiar* at the scene of the atrocity.

There was something in his manner of emphasizing the word *"peculiar,"* which caused me to shudder, without knowing why.

"No, nothing *peculiar,"* I said; "nothing more, at least, than we both saw stated in the paper."

"The *Gazette,"* he replied, "has not entered, I fear, into the unusual horror of the thing. But dismiss the idle opinions of this print. It appears to me that this mystery is considered insoluble, for the very reason which should cause it to be regarded as easy of solution —I mean for the *outré* character of its features. The police are confounded by the seeming absence of motive —not for the murder itself—but for the atrocity of the murder. They are puzzled, too, by the seeming impossibility of reconciling the voices heard in contention, with the facts that no one was discovered upstairs but the assassinated Mademoiselle L'Espanaye, and that there were no means of egress without the notice of the party ascending.

"I am now awaiting," continued he, looking toward the door of our apartment—"I am now awaiting a person who, although perhaps not the perpetrator of these butcheries, must have been in some measure implicated in their perpetration. Of the worst portion of the crimes committed, it is probable that he is innocent. I hope that I am right in this supposition; for upon it I build my expectation of reading the entire riddle. I look for the man here—in this room—every moment. It is true that he may not arrive; but the probability is that he will. Should he come, it will be necessary to detain him. Here are pistols; and we both know how to use them when occasion demands their use."

I took the pistols, scarcely knowing what I did, or believing what I heard, while Dupin went on, very much as if in a soliloquy.

"That the voices heard in contention," he said, "by the party upon the stairs, were not the voices of the women themselves, was fully proved by the evidence. Murder, then, has been committed by some third party; and the voices of this third party were those heard in contention. Let me now advert—not to the whole testimony respecting these voices—but to what was *peculiar* in that testimony. Did you observe any thing peculiar about it? Anything that seems a bit strange?"

I remarked that, while all the witnesses agreed in supposing the gruff voice to be that of a Frenchman, there was much disagreement in regard to the shrill, or, as one individual termed it, the harsh voice.

"That was the evidence itself," said Dupin, "but it was not the peculiarity of the evidence. You have observed nothing distinctive. Yet there *was* something to be observed. The witnesses, as you remark, agreed about the gruff voice; they were here unanimous. But in regard to the shrill voice, the peculiarity is—not that they disagreed—but that, while an Italian, an Englishman, a Spaniard, a Hollander, and a Frenchman attempted to describe it, each one spoke of it as that *of a foreigner.* Each is sure that it was not the voice of one of his own countrymen. Each likens it—not to the voice of an individual of any nation with whose language he is conversant—but the converse. Now, how strangely unusual must that voice have really been, about which such testimony as this *could* have been elicited!—in whose *tones,* even, denizens of the five great divisions of Europe could recognize nothing familiar! You will say that it might have been the voice of an Asiatic—of an African. Neither Asiatics nor Africans abound in Paris; but, without denying the inference, I will now merely call your attention to three points. The voice is termed by one witness 'harsh rather than shrill.' It is represented by two others to have been 'quick and *unequal.*' No words—no sounds resembling words—were by any witness mentioned as distinguishable.

"I know not," continued Dupin, "what impression I may have made, so far, upon your own understanding; but I do not hesitate to say that legitimate deductions even from this portion of the testimony—the portion respecting the gruff and shrill voices—are in themselves sufficient to engender a suspicion which should give direction to all farther progress in the investigation of the mystery. What the suspicion is, however, I will not say just yet. I merely wish you to bear in mind that, with myself, it was sufficiently forcible to give a definite form —a certain tendency—to my inquiries in the chamber.

"Let us now transport ourselves, in fancy, to this chamber. What shall we first seek here? The means of egress employed by the murderers.

"There are two windows in the chamber. One of them is unobstructed by furniture, and is wholly visible. The lower portion of the other is hidden from view by the head of the unwieldy bedstead which is thrust close up against it. The former was found securely fastened from within. It resisted the utmost force of those who endeavored to raise it. A large gimlet-hole had been pierced in its frame to the left, and a very stout nail was found fitted therein, nearly to the head. Upon examining the other window, a similar nail was seen similarly fitted in it; and a vigorous attempt to raise this sash failed also.

"The murderers *did* escape from one of these windows. This being so, they could not have re-fastened the sashes from the inside. Yet the sashes *were* fastened. They *must,* then, have the power of fastening themselves. There was no escape from this conclusion. I stepped to the unobstructed casement, withdrew the nail with some difficulty, and attempted to raise the sash. It resisted all my efforts, as I had anticipated. A careful search soon brought to light the hidden spring. I pressed it, and, satisfied with the discovery, forbore to upraise the sash.

"I now replaced the nail and regarded it attentively. A person passing out through this window might have reclosed it, and the spring would have caught—but the nail could not have been replaced. The conclusion was plain, and again narrowed in the field of my investigations. The assassins *must* have escaped through the other window. Supposing, then, the springs upon each sash to be the same, as was probable, there *must* be found a difference between the nails, or at least between the modes of their fixture. Getting upon the sacking of the bedstead, I looked over the head-board minutely at the second casement. Passing my hand down behind the board, I readily discovered and pressed the spring, which was, as I had supposed, identical in character with its neighbor. I now looked at the nail. It was as stout as the other, and apparently fitted in the same manner—driven in nearly up to the head.

"You will say that I was puzzled; but, if you think so, you must have misunderstood the nature of the inductions. I had traced the secret to its ultimate result,—and that result was *the nail.* It had, I say, in every respect, the appearance of its fellow in the other window; but this fact was an absolute nullity (conclusive as it might seem to be) when compared with the consideration that here, at this point, terminated the clew. 'There *must* be something wrong,' I said, 'about the nail.' I touched it; and the head, with about a quarter of an inch of the shank, came off in my fingers. The rest of the shank was in the gimlet-hole, where it had been broken off. The fracture was an old one (for its edges were incrusted with rust), and had apparently been accomplished by the blow of a hammer, which had partially imbedded, in the top of the bottom sash, the head portion of the nail. I now carefully replaced this head portion in the indentation whence I had taken it, and the resemblance to a perfect nail was complete—the fissure was invisible. Pressing the spring, I gently raised the sash for a few inches; the head went up with it, remaining firm in its bed. I closed the window, and the semblance of the whole nail was again perfect.

"This riddle, so far, was now unriddled. The assassin had escaped through the window which looked upon the bed. Dropping of its own accord upon his exit (or perhaps purposely closed), it had become fastened by the spring; and it was the retention of this spring which had been mistaken by the police for that of the nail,— farther inquiry being thus considered unnecessary.

"The next question is that of the mode of descent. Upon this point I had been satisfied in my walk with you around the building. About five feet and a half from the casement in question there runs a lightning-rod. From this rod it would have been impossible for any one to reach the window itself, to say nothing of entering it. I observed, however, that the shutters of the fourth story were of the peculiar kind called by Parisian carpenters *ferrades*. It was clear to me that the shutter belonging to the window at the head of the bed, would, if swung fully back to the wall, reach to within two feet of the lightning-rod. It was also evident that, by exertion of a very unusual degree of activity and courage, an entrance into the window, from the rod, might have been thus effected. By reaching to the distance of two feet and a half (we now suppose the shutter open to its whole extent) a robber might have taken a firm grasp upon the trellis-work. Letting go, then, his hold upon the rod, placing his feet securely against the wall, and springing boldly from it, he might have swung the shutter so as to close it, and, if we imagine the window open at the time, might even have swung himself into the room.

"I wish you to bear especially in mind that I have spoken of a *very* unusual degree of activity as requisite to success in so hazardous and so difficult a feat. It is my design to show you first, that the thing might possibly have been accomplished:—but, secondly and *chiefly,* I wish to impress upon your understanding the *very extra-ordinary*—the almost praeternatural character of that agility which could have accomplished it."

At these words a vague and half-formed conception of the meaning of Dupin flitted over my mind. I seemed to be upon the verge of comprehension, without power to comprehend—as men, at times, find themselves upon the brink of remembrance, without being able, in the end, to remember. My friend went on with his discourse.

"You will see," he said, "that I have shifted the question from the mode of egress to that of ingress. It was my design to convey the idea that both were effected in the same manner, at the same point. Let us now revert to the interior of the room. Let us survey the appearances here. The drawers of the bureau, it is said, had been rifled, although many articles of apparel still remained within them. Those found were at least of as good quality as any likely to be possessed by Madame L'Espanaye and her daughter. If a thief had taken any, why didn't he take the best? And why did he abandon four thousand francs in gold to encumber himself with a bundle of linen? The gold *was* abandoned. Nearly the whole sum mentioned by Monsieur Mignaud, the banker, was discovered, in bags, upon the floor. I wish you therefore, to discard from your thoughts the blundering idea of *motive,* engendered in the brains of the police by that portion of the evidence which speaks of money delivered at the door of the house a few days earlier.

"Keeping now steadily in mind the points to which I have drawn your attention—that peculiar voice, that unusual agility, and that startling absence of motive in a murder so singularly atrocious as this—let us glance at the butchery itself. Here is a woman strangled to death by manual strength, and thrust up a chimney head downward. Ordinary assassins employ no such mode of murder as this. Least of all, do they thus dispose of the murdered. In the manner of thrusting the corpse up the chimney, you will admit that there was something *excessively outré*—something altogther irreconcilable with our common notions of human action, even when we suppose the actors the most depraved of men. Think, too, how great must have been that strength which could have thrust the body *up* such an aperture so forcibly that the united vigor of several persons was found barely sufficient to drag it *down!*

"Turn, now, to other indications of the employment of a vigor most marvellous. On the hearth were thick tresses—very thick tresses—of gray human hair. These had been torn out by the roots. You are aware of the great force necessary in tearing thus from the head even twenty or thirty hairs together. You saw the locks in question as well as myself. Their roots (a hideous sight!) were clotted with fragments of the flesh of the scalp—sure token of the prodigious power which had been exerted in uprooting perhaps half a million of hairs at a time. The throat of the old lady was not merely cut, but the head absolutely severed from the body: the instrument was a mere razor. I wish you also to look at the *brutal* ferocity of these deeds. Of the bruises upon the body of Madame L'Espanaye I do not speak. Monsieur Dumas, and his worthy coadjutor Monsieur Etienne, have pronounced that they were inflicted by some obtuse instrument; and so far these gentlemen are very correct. The obtuse instrument was clearly the stone pavement in the yard, upon which the victim had fallen from the window which looked in upon the bed. This idea, however simple it may now seem, escaped the police for the same reason that the breadth of the shutters escaped them—because, by the affair of the nails, their perceptions had been hermetically sealed against the possibility of the windows having ever been opened at all. Then, do you see what follows?

"If now, in addition to all these things, you have properly reflected upon the odd disorder of the chamber, we have gone so far as to combine the ideas of an agility astounding, a strength superhuman, a ferocity brutal, a butchery without motive, a *grotesquerie* in horror absolutely alien from humanity, and a voice foreign in tone to the ears of men of many nations, and devoid of all distinct or intelligible syllabification. What result, then, has ensued? What impression have I made upon your fancy?"

I felt a creeping of the flesh as Dupin asked me the question. "A madman," I said, "has done this deed —some raving maniac, escaped from a neighboring *Maison de Santé.*"

"In some respects," he replied, "your idea is not irrelevant. But the voices of madmen, even in their wildest paroxysms, are never found to tally with that peculiar voice heard upon the stairs. Madmen are of some nation, and their language, however incoherent in its words, has always the coherence of syllabification. Besides, the hair of a madman is not such as I now hold in my hand. I disentangled this little tuft from the rigidly clutched fingers of Madame L'Espanaye. Tell me what you can make of it."

"Dupin!" I said, completely unnerved; "this hair is most unusual—this is no *human* hair."

"I have not asserted that it is," said he; "but, before we decide this point, I wish you to glance at the little sketch I have here traced upon this paper. It is a *facsimile* draw-

ing of what has been described in one portion of the
testimony as 'dark bruises and deep indentations of
finger nails' upon the throat of Mademoiselle L'Espanaye, and in another (by Messrs. Dumas and Etienne)
as a 'series of livid spots, evidently the impression of
fingers.'

"You will perceive," continued my friend, spreading
out the paper upon the table before us, "that this drawing gives the idea of a firm and fixed hold. There is no
slipping apparent. Each finger has retained—possibly
until the death of the victim—the fearful grasp by which
it originally imbedded itself. Attempt, now, to place all
your fingers, at the same time, in the respecting impres-
sions as you see them."

I made the attempt in vain.

"We are possibly not giving this matter a fair trial,"
he said. "The paper is spread out upon a plane surface;
but the human throat is cylindrical. Here is a billet of
wood, the circumference of which is about that of the
throat. Wrap the drawing around it, and try the experi-
ment again."

I did so; but the difficulty was even more obvious
than before. "This," I said, "is the mark of no human
hand."

"Read now," replied Dupin, "this passage from
Cuvier."

It was a minute anatomical and generally descriptive
account of the large fulvous ourang-outang of the East
Indian Islands. The gigantic stature, the prodigious
strength and activity, the wild ferocity, and the imitative

propensities of these mammalia are sufficiently well known to all. I understood the full horrors of the murder at once.

"The description of the digits," said I, as I made an end of the reading, "is in exact accordance with this drawing. I see that no animal but an ourang-outang, of the species here mentioned, could have impressed the indentations as you have traced them. This tuft of tawny hair, too, is identical in character with that of the beast of Cuvier. But I cannot possibly comprehend the particulars of this frightful mystery. Besides, there were *two* voices heard in contention, and one of them was unquestionably the voice of a Frenchman."

"True; and you will remember an expression attributed almost unanimously, by the evidence, to this voice, —the expression, '*mon Dieu!*' This, under the circumstances, has been justly characterized by one of the witnesses (Montani, the confectioner) as an expression of remonstrance or expostulation. Upon these two words, therefore, I have mainly built my hopes of a full solution of the riddle. A Frenchman was cognizant of the murder. It is possible—indeed it is far more than probable— that he was innocent of all participation in the bloody transactions which took place. The ourang-outang may have escaped from him. He may have traced it to the chamber; but, under the agitating circumstances which ensued, he could never have recaptured it. It is still at large. I will not pursue these guesses—for I have no right to call them more—since the shades of reflection upon which they are based are scarcely of sufficient depths to be appreciable by my own intellect, and since I could not pretend to make them intelligible to the understanding of another. We will call them guesses, then, and speak of them as such. If the Frenchman in question is indeed, as I suppose, innocent of this atrocity, this advertisement, which I left last night, upon our return home, at the office of *Le Monde* (a paper devoted to the shipping interest, and much sought by sailors), will bring him to our residence."

He handed me a paper, and I read thus:

"CAUGHT—*In the Bois de Boulogne, early in the morning of the —— inst.* (the morning of the murder), *a very large, tawny ourang-outang of the Bornese species. The owner (who is ascertained to be a sailor, belonging to a Maltese vessel) may have the animal again, upon identifying it satisfactorily, and paying a few charges arising from its capture and keeping. Call at No. —— Rue ——, Faubourg St. Germain — au troisième.*"

"How was it possible," I asked, "that you should know the man to be a sailor, and belonging to a Maltese vessel?"

"I do *not* know it," said Dupin. "I am not *sure* of it. Here, however, is a small piece of ribbon, which from its form, and from its greasy appearance, has evidently been used in tying the hair in one of those long *queues* of which sailors are so fond. Moreover, this knot is one which few besides sailors can tie, and is peculiar to the Maltese. I picked the ribbon up at the foot of the lightning-rod. It could not have belonged to either of the deceased. Now if, after all, I am wrong in my induction from this ribbon, that the Frenchman was a sailor belonging to a Maltese vessel, still I can have done no harm in saying what I did in the advertisement. If I am in error, he will merely suppose that I have been misled by some circumstance into which he will not take the trouble to inquire. But if I am right, a great point is gained. Cognizant although innocent of the murder, the Frenchman will naturally hesitate about replying to the advertisement—about demanding the ourang-outang. He will reason thus:—'I am innocent; I am poor; my ourang-outang is of great value—to one in my circumstances a fortune of itself—why should I lose it through idle apprehensions of danger? Here it is, within my grasp. It was found in the Bois de Boulogne—at a vast distance from the scene of that butchery. How can it ever be suspected that a brute beast should have done the deed? The police are at fault—they have failed to procure the slightest clew. Should they even trace the animal, it would be impossible to prove me cognizant of the murder, or to implicate me in guilt on account of that cognizance. Above all, *I am known.* The advertiser designates me as the possessor of the beast. I am not sure to what limit his knowledge may extend. Should I avoid claiming a property of so great value, which it is known that I possess, I will render the animal at least, liable to suspicion. It is not my policy to attract attention either to myself or to the beast. I will answer the advertisement, get the ourang-outang, and keep it close until this matter has blown over.' "

At this moment we heard a step upon the stairs.

"Be ready," said Dupin, "with your pistols, but neither use them nor show them until at a signal from myself."

The front door of the house had been left open, and the visitor had entered, without ringing, and advanced several steps upon the staircase. Now, however, he seemed to hesitate. Presently we heard him descending. Dupin was moving quickly to the door, when we again heard him coming up. He did not turn back a second time, but stepped up with decision, and rapped at the door of our chamber.

"Come in," said Dupin, in a cheerful and hearty tone.

A man entered. He was a sailor, evidently,—a tall, stout, and muscular-looking person, with a certain dare-devil expression of countenance, not altogther unprepossessing. His face, greatly sunburnt, was more than half hidden by whisker and *mustachio.* He had with him a huge oaken cudgel, but appeared to be otherwise unarmed. He bowed awkwardly, and bade us "good evening," in French accents, which, although somewhat Neufchatelish, were still sufficiently indicative of a Parisian origin.

"Sit down, my friend," said Dupin. "I suppose you have called about the ourang- outang. Upon my word, I almost envy you the possession of him; a remarkably fine, and no doubt a very valuable animal. How old do you suppose him to be?"

The sailor drew a long breath, with the air of a man relieved of some intolerable burden, and then replied, calmly enough, and in an assured tone:

"I have no way of telling—but he can't be more than four or five years old. Have you got him here?"

"Oh, no; we had no conveniences for keeping him here. He is at a livery stable in the Rue Dubourg, just by. You can get him in the morning. Of course you are prepared to identify the property?"

"To be sure I am, sir."

"I shall be sorry to part with him," said Dupin.

"I don't mean that you should be at all this trouble for nothing, sir," said the man. "Couldn't expect it. Am very willing to pay a reward for the finding of the animal—that is to say, any thing in reason."

"Well," replied my friend, "that is all very fair, to be sure. Let me think!—what should I have? Oh! I will tell you. My reward shall be this. You shall give me all the information in your power about these murders in the Rue Morgue."

Dupin said the last words in a very low tone, and very quietly. Just as quietly, too, he walked toward the door, locked it, and put the key in his pocket. He then drew a pistol from his bosom and placed it, without the least flurry, upon the table.

The sailor's face flushed up as if he were struggling with suffocation. He started to his feet and grasped his cudgel; but the next moment he fell back into his seat, trembling violently, and with the countenance of death itself. He spoke not a word. I pitied him from the bottom of my heart. Terror is always most pitiable.

"My friend," said Dupin, in a kind tone, "you are

alarming yourself unnecessarily—you are indeed. We mean you no harm whatever. I pledge you the honor of a gentleman, and of a Frenchman, that we intend you no injury. I perfectly well know that you are innocent of the atrocities in the Rue Morgue. It will not do, however, to deny that you are in some measure implicated in them. From what I have already said, you must know that I have had means of information about this matter —means of which you could never have dreamed. Now the thing stands thus. You have done nothing which you could have avoided—nothing, certainly, which renders you culpable. You were not even guilty of robbery, when you might have robbed with impunity. You have nothing to conceal. You have no reason for concealment. On the other hand, you are bound by every principle of honor to confess all you know. An innocent man is now imprisoned, charged with that crime of which you can point out the perpetrator."

The sailor had recovered his presence of mind, in a great measure, while Dupin uttered these words; but his original boldness of bearing was all gone.

"So help me God!" said he, after a brief pause, "I *will* tell you all I know about this affair;—but I do not expect you to believe one half I say—I would be a fool indeed if I did. Still, I *am* innocent, and I will make a clean breast if I die for it."

What he stated was, in substance, this. He had lately made a voyage to the Indian Archipelago. A party, of which he formed one, landed at Borneo, and passed into the interior on an excursion of pleasure. Himself and a companion had captured the ourang-outang. This companion dying, the animal fell into his own exclusive possession. After great trouble, occasioned by the intractable ferocity of his captive during the home voyage, he at length succeeded in lodging it safely at his own residence in Paris, where, not to attract toward himself the unpleasant curiosity of his neighbors, he kept it carefully secluded, until such time as it should recover from a wound in the foot, received from a splinter on board ship. His ultimate design was to sell it.

Returning home from some sailors' frolic on the night, or rather in the morning, of the murder, he found the beast occupying his own bedroom, into which it had broken from a closet adjoining, where it had been, as was thought, securely confined. Razor in hand, and fully lathered, it was sitting before a looking-glass, attempting the operation of shaving, in which it had no doubt previously watched its master through the keyhole of the closet. Terrified at the sight of so dangerous a weapon in the possession of an animal so ferocious, and so well able to use it, the man, for some moments, was at a loss what to do. He had been accustomed, however, to quiet the creature, even in its fiercest moods, by the use of a whip, and to this he now resorted. Upon sight of it, the ourang-outang sprang at once through the door of the chamber, down the stairs, and thence, through a window, unfortunately open, into the street.

The Frenchman followed in despair; the ape, razor still in hand, occasionally stopping to look back and gesticulate at his pursuer, until the latter had nearly

come up with it. It then again made off. In this manner
the chase continued for a long time. The streets were
profoundly quiet, as it was nearly three o'clock in the
morning. In passing down an alley in the rear of the
Rue Morgue, the fugitive's attention was arrested by a
light gleaming from the open window of Madame
L'Espanaye's chamber, in the fourth story of her house.
Rushing to the building, it perceived the lightning-rod,
clambered up with inconceivable agility, grasped the
shutter, which was thrown fully back against the wall,
and, by its means, swung itself directly upon the head-
board of the bed. The whole feat did not occupy a minute. The shutter was kicked open again by the ourang-
outang as it entered the room.

The sailor, in the meantime, was both rejoiced and
perplexed. He had strong hopes of now recapturing
the brute, as it could scarcely escape from the trap into
which it had ventured, except by the rod, where it might
be intercepted as it came down. On the other hand, there
was much cause for anxiety as to what it might do in the
house. This latter reflection urged the man still to follow
the fugitive. A lightning-rod is ascended without difficulty, especially by a sailor; but, when he had arrived
as high as the window, which lay far to his left, his career
was stopped; the most that he could accomplish was to
reach over so as to obtain a glimpse of the interior of the
room. At this glimpse he nearly fell from his hold
through excess of horror. Now it was that those hideous
shrieks arose upon the night, which had startled from
slumber the inmates of the Rue Morgue. Madame

L'Espanaye and her daughter, habited in their night clothes, had apparently been occupied in arranging some papers in the iron chest already mentioned, which had been wheeled into the middle of the room. It was open, and its contents lay beside it on the floor. The victims must have been sitting with their backs toward the window; and, from the time elapsing between the ingress of the beast and the screams, it seems probable that it was not immediately perceived. The flapping-to of the shutter would naturally have been attributed to the wind.

As the sailor looked in, the gigantic animal had seized Madame L'Espanaye by the hair (which was loose, as she had been combing it), and was flourishing the razor about her face, in imitation of the motions of a barber. The daughter lay prostrate and motionless; she had swooned. The screams and struggles of the old lady (during which the hair was torn from her head) had the effect of changing the probably pacific purposes of the ourang- outang into those of wrath. With one determined sweep of its muscular arm it nearly severed her head from her body. The sight of blood inflamed its anger into frenzy. Gnashing its teeth, and flashing fire from its eyes, it flew upon the body of the girl, and imbedded its fearful talons in her throat, retaining its grasp until she expired. Its wandering and wild glances fell at this moment upon the head of the bed, over which the face of its master, rigid with horror, was just discernible. The fury of the beast, who no doubt bore still in mind the dreaded whip, was instantly converted into fear. Conscious of having deserved punishment, it seemed desirous of concealing its bloody deeds, and skipped about the chamber in an agony of nervous agitation; throwing down and breaking the furniture as it moved, and dragging the bed from the bedstead. In conclusion, it seized first the corpse of the daughter, and thrust it up the chimney, as it was found; then that of the old lady, which it immediately hurled through the window headlong.

As the ape approached the casement with its mutilated burden, the sailor shrank aghast to the rod, and, rather gliding than clambering down it, hurried at once home—dreading the consequences of the butchery, and gladly abandoning, in his terror, all solicitude about the fate of the ourang- outang. The words heard by the party upon the staircase were the Frenchman's exclamations of horror and affright, commingled with the fiendish jabbering of the brute.

I have scarcely any thing to add. The ourang- outang must have escaped from the chamber, by the rod, just before the breaking of the door. It must have closed the window as it passed through it. It was subsequently caught by the owner himself, who obtained for it a very large sum at the *Jardin des Plantes.* Le Bon was instantly released, upon our narration of the circumstances (with some comments from Dupin) at the *bureau* of the Prefect of Police. This functionary, however well disposed to my friend, could not altogether conceal his chagrin at the turn which affairs had taken.

It took

THE TELL-TALE HEART

to proclaim a murder

It is impossible to say how first the idea entered my brain; but once conceived, it haunted me day and night. Object there was none. Passion there was none. I loved the old man. He had never wronged me. He had never given me insult. For his gold I had no desire. I think it was his eye! Yes, it was this! One of his eyes resembled that of a vulture—a pale blue eye, with a film over it. Whenever it fell upon me, my blood ran cold; and so by degrees—very gradually— I made up my mind to take the life of the old man, and thus rid myself of the eye forever.

Now this is the point. You fancy me mad. Madmen know nothing. But you should have seen *me*. You should have seen how wisely I proceeded—with what

caution—with what foresight—with what dissimulation
I went to work! I was never kinder to the old man
than during the whole week before I killed him. And
every night, about midnight, I turned the latch of his
door and opened it—oh, so gently! And then, when I
had made an opening sufficient for my head, I put in
a dark lantern, all closed, closed, so that no light shone
out, and then I thrust in my head. Oh, you would have
laughed to see how cunningly I thrust it in! I moved
it slowly--very, very slowly, so that I might not dis-
turb the old man's sleep. It took me an hour to place
my whole head within the opening so far that I could
see him as he lay upon his bed. Ha!—would a madman
have been so wise as this? And then, when my head
was well in the room, I undid the lantern cautiously—
oh, so cautiously—cautiously (for the hinges creaked)
—I undid it just so much that a single thin ray fell
upon the vulture eye. And this I did for seven long
nights—every night just at midnight—but I found the
eye always closed. And so it was impossible to do the
work; for it was not the old man who vexed me, but
his Evil Eye. And every morning, when the day broke,
I went boldly into the chamber, and spoke courageous-
ly to him, calling him by name in a hearty tone, and
inquiring how he had passed the night.

Upon the eighth night I was more than usually cautious in opening the door. A watch's minute hand
moves more quickly than did mine. Never before that
night had I felt the extent of my own powers!

I had my head in, and was about to open the lantern, when my thumb slipped upon the tin fastening, and the old man sprang up in the bed, crying out—"Who's there?"

I kept quite still and said nothing. For a whole hour I did not move a muscle, and in the meantime I did not hear him lie down. He was still sitting up in the bed listening;—just as I have done, night after night, hearkening to the death watches in the wall.

When I had waited a long time, very patiently, without hearing him lie down, I resolved to open a little—a very, very little crevice in the lantern. So I opened it—you cannot imagine how stealthily, stealthily—until, at length, a single dim ray, like the thread of a spider, shot from out the crevice and full upon the vulture eye.

It was open—wide, wide open—and I grew furious as I gazed upon it. I saw it with perfect distinctness—all a dull blue, with a hideous veil over it that chilled the very marrow in my bones. But I could see nothing else of the old man's face or person: for I had directed the ray as if by instinct, precisely upon the evil eye.

Then there came to my ears a low, dull, quick sound, such as a watch makes when enveloped in cotton. I knew *that* sound well, too. It was the beating of the old man's heart. It increased my fury, as the beating of a drum stimulates the soldier into courage.

But even yet I refrained and kept still. I scarcely breathed. I held the lantern motionless. I tried how steadily I could maintain the ray upon the eye. Meantime the hellish tattoo of the heart increased. It grew quicker and quicker, and louder and louder every instant. The old man's terror *must* have been extreme! It grew louder, I say, louder every moment. Amid the dreadful silence of that old house, so strange a noise as this excited me to uncontrollable terror. Yet, for some minutes longer I refrained and stood still. But the beating grew louder, louder! I thought the heart must burst. And now a new anxiety seized me—the sound would be heard by a neighbor! The old man's hour had come! With a loud yell, I threw open the lantern and leaped into the room. He shrieked once— once only. In an instant I dragged him to the floor, and pulled the heavy bed over him. I then smiled gaily, to find the deed so far done. But, for many minutes, the heart beat on with a muffled sound. This, however, did not vex me; it would not be heard through the wall. At length it ceased. The old man was dead. I removed the bed and examined the corpse. Yes, he was stone, stone dead. I placed my hand upon the heart and held it there many minutes. There was no pulsation. He was stone dead. His eye would trouble me no more.

If you still think me mad, you will think so no longer when I describe the wise precautions I took for the concealment of the body. The night waned, and I worked hastily, but in silence. First of all I dismembered the corpse. I cut off the head and the arms and the legs.

I then took up three planks from the flooring of the chamber, and deposited all between the scantlings. I then replaced the boards so cleverly, so cunningly, that

no human eye—not even *his*—could have detected anything wrong. There was nothing to wash out—no stain
of any kind—no blood-spot whatever. I had been too
wary for that. A tub had caught all—ha! ha!

When I had made an end of these labors, it was
four o'clock—still dark as midnight. As the bell
sounded the hour, there came a knocking at the street
door. I went down to open it with a light heart —for
what had I *now* to fear? There entered three men, who
introduced themselves with perfect suavity as officers
of the police. A shriek had been heard by a neighbor
during the night; suspicion of foul play had been
aroused; information had been lodged at the police
office, and they (the officers) had been deputed to
search the premises.

I smiled —for *what* had I to fear? I bade the gentlemen welcome. The shriek, I said, was my own in a
dream. The old man, I mentioned, was absent in the
country. I took my visitors all over the house. I bade
them search—search *well*. I led them, at length, to *his*
chamber. I showed them his treasures, secure, undisturbed. In the enthusiasm of my confidence, I brought
chairs into the room, and desired them *here* to rest
from their fatigues, while I myself, in the wild audacity
of my perfect triumph, placed my own seat upon the
very spot beneath which reposed the corpse of the
victim.

The officers were satisfied. My *manner* had convinced them. I was singularly at ease. They sat, and
while I answered cheerily, they chatted familiar things.

But, ere long, I felt myself getting pale and wished them gone. My head ached, and I fancied a ringing in my ears; but still they sat and still chatted. The ringing became more distinct; it continued and became more distinct. I talked more freely to get rid of the feeling; but it continued and gained definitiveness—until, at length, I found that the noise was *not* within my ears.

No doubt I now grew *very* pale;—but I talked more fluently and with a heightened voice. Yet the sound increased—and what could I do? It was *a low, dull, quick sound—much such a sound as a watch makes when enveloped in cotton.* I gasped for breath—and yet the officers heard it not. I talked more quickly—more vehemently; but the noise steadily increased. I arose and argued about trifles, in a high key and with violent gesticulations, but the noise steadily increased. Why *would* they not be gone? I paced the floor to and fro with heavy strides, as if excited to fury by the observation of the men—but the noise steadily increased. Oh God! what *could* I do? I foamed—I raved —I swore! I swung the chair upon which I had been sitting, and grated it upon the boards, but the noise arose over all and continually increased. It grew louder —louder—*louder!* And still the men chatted pleasantly, and smiled. Was it possible they heard not? Almighty God!—no, no! They heard!—they suspected!—they *knew!*—they were making a mockery of my horror!— this I thought, and this I think. But anything was better than this agony! Anything was more tolerable than this derision! I could bear those hypocritical smiles no longer! I felt that I must scream or die!—and now —again!—hark! louder! louder! louder! *louder!*—

"Villains!" I shrieked, "dissemble no more! I admit the deed!—tear up the planks!—here, here!—it is the beating of his hideous heart!"

AMBROSE BIERCE

. . . was born in Ohio, the youngest of nine children. His only formal schooling came during a year spent at the Kentucky Military Academy. After the Civil War, in which he served with distinction, he moved to California and embarked on a career as a journalist. Though he lived for a time in London and in Washington, he always considered California his home. Through a daily (and later Sunday) column he wrote for William Randolph Hearst's "San Francisco Examiner," Bierce aired his strong and opinionated views on books and writers, and became widely known and feared as the literary dictator of the Pacific Coast.

Meanwhile his collections of short stories were bringing him a wider fame. He has been recognized as a writer in the direct tradition of Edgar Allan Poe, and like Poe, was "a master of brevity in horror." His skill and artistry in building suspense and terror out of seemingly ordinary events is perfectly demonstrated in "The Damned Thing."

Wanted for murder

THE DAMNED THING

baffled a jury

BY THE LIGHT of a tallow candle which had been placed on one end of a rough table, a man was reading something written in a book. It was an old account book, greatly worn; and the writing was not very legible, for the man sometimes held the page close to the flame of the candle to get a stronger light on it. The shadow of the book would then throw into obscurity half of the room, darkening a number of faces and figures; for besides the reader, eight other men were present.

Seven of them sat against the rough log walls, silent, motionless, and, the room being small, not very far from the table. By extending an arm any one of them could have touched the eighth man, who lay on the table, face upward, partly covered by a sheet, his arms at his sides. He was dead.

The person reading was the coroner. It was by virtue of his office that he had possession of the book in which he was reading; it had been found among the dead man's effects—in his cabin, where the inquest was now taking place.

When the coroner had finished reading, he put the book into his breast pocket. At that moment the door was pushed open and a young man entered. He, clearly, was not of mountain birth and breeding: he was clad as those who dwell in cities. His clothing was dusty, however, as from travel. He had, in fact, been riding hard to attend the inquest.

The coroner nodded; no one one else greeted him

The young man smiled. "I am sorry to have kept you," he said. "I went away, not to evade your summons, but to send to my newspaper an account of what I suppose I am called back to relate."

The coroner smiled.

"The account that you sent to your newspaper," he said, "probably differs from that which you will give here under oath."

"That," replied the other, rather hotly and with a visible flush, "is as you please. I have a copy of what I sent. It was not written as news, for it is incredible, but as fiction. It may go as a part of my testimony under oath."

"But you say it is incredible."

"That is nothing to you, if I also swear it is true."

The coroner was silent for a time, his eyes upon the floor. The men about the sides of the cabin talked in whispers, but seldom withdrew their gaze from the face of the corpse. Presently the coroner lifted his eyes and said: "We will resume the inquest."

The men removed their hats. The witness was sworn.

"What is your name?" the coroner asked.

"William Harker."

"Age?"

"Twenty-seven."

"You knew the deceased, Hugh Morgan?"

"Yes."

"You were with him when he died?"

"Near him."

"How did that happen—your presence, I mean?"

"I was visiting him at his place, to shoot and fish. Part of my purpose, however, was to study him and his odd, solitary way of life. He seemed a good model for a character in fiction. I sometimes write stories."

"I sometimes read them."

"Thank you."

"Stories in general—not yours."

Some of the jurors laughed.

"Relate the circumstances of this man's death," said the coroner. "You may use any notes you please."

The witness understood. He held a manuscript near the candle and, turning the leaves until he found the passage that he wanted, began to read.

"... The sun had hardly risen when we left the house. We were looking for quail, each with a shotgun, but we had only one dog. Morgan said that our best ground was beyond a certain ridge that he pointed out, and we crossed it by a trail through the chaparral. On the other side was comparatively level ground, thickly covered with wild oats. As we emerged from the chaparral Morgan was but a few yards in advance. Suddenly we heard, at a little distance to our right and partly in front, a noise as of some animal thrashing about in the bushes, which we could see were violently agitated.

" 'We've startled a deer,' I said. 'I wish we had brought a rifle.'

"Morgan, who had stopped and was intently watching the agitated chaparral, said nothing, but had cocked both barrels of his gun and was holding it in readiness to aim. I thought him a trifle excited, which surprised me, for he had a reputation for exceptional coolness, even in moments of sudden and imminent peril.

" 'Oh, come,' I said. 'You are not going to fill up a deer with quail-shot, are you?'

"Still he did not reply; but catching sight of his face as he turned it slightly toward me, I was struck by the intensity of his look. Then I understood that we had serious business in hand, and my first conjecture was that we had 'jumped' a grizzly. I advanced to Morgan's side, cocking my gun as I moved.

"The bushes were now quiet and the sounds had ceased, but Morgan was as attentive to the place as before.

" 'What is it? What the devil is it?' I asked.

" 'That Damned Thing!' he replied, without turning

his head. His voice was husky and unnatural. He trembled visibly.

"I was about to speak further, when I observed the wild oats near the place of the disturbance moving in the most inexplicable way. I can hardly describe it. The grain seemed to be stirred by a streak of wind, which not only bent it, but pressed it down—crushed it so that it did not rise; and this movement was slowly prolonging itself directly toward us.

"Nothing that I had ever seen had affected me so strangely as this unfamiliar and unaccountable phenomenon, yet I am unable to recall any sense of fear. However, the apparently causeless movement of the grain, and the slow, undeviating approach of the line of disturbance were distinctly disquieting.

"My companion appeared actually frightened, and I could hardly credit my senses when I saw him suddenly lift his gun to his shoulder and fire both barrels at the agitated grain! Before the smoke of the discharge had cleared away, I heard a loud savage cry—a scream like that of a wild animal. Flinging his gun on the ground, Morgan sprang away and ran swiftly from the spot. At the same instant I was thrown violently to the ground by the impact of something unseen in the smoke—some soft, heavy substance that seemed thrown against me with great force.

"Before I could get on my feet and recover my gun, which seemed to have been struck from my hands, I heard Morgan crying out as if in mortal agony, and mingling with his cries were such hoarse, savage sounds as one hears from fighting dogs. Inexpressibly terrified, I struggled to my feet and looked in the direction of Morgan's retreat; may Heaven in mercy spare me from another sight like that!

"At a distance of less than thirty yards was my friend, down upon one knee, his head thrown back at a frightful angle, hatless, his long hair in disorder, and his whole body in violent movement from side to side, backward and forward. His right arm was lifted and seemed to lack the hand—at least, I could see none. The other arm was invisible.

"At times, as my memory now reports this extraordinary scene, I could discern but a part of his body; it was as if he had been partly blotted out—I cannot otherwise express it—then a shifting of his position would bring it all into view again.

"All this must have occurred within a few seconds, yet in that time Morgan assumed all the postures of a determined wrestler vanquished by superior weight and strength. I saw nothing but him, and him not always distinctly. During the entire incident his shouts and curses were heard, as if through an enveloping uproar of such sounds of rage and fury as I had never heard from the throat of man or brute!

"For a moment only I stood irresolute, then throwing down my gun I ran forward to my friend's assistance. I had a vague belief that he was suffering from a fit, or some form of convulsion. Before I could reach his side, he was prone and quiet.

"All sounds had ceased, but with a feeling of such

terror as even these awful events had not inspired I now saw again the mysterious movement of the wild oats, prolonging itself from the trampled area about the prostrate man toward the edge of the wood. It was only when it had reached the wood that I was able to withdraw my eyes and look at my companion. He was dead."

The coroner rose from his seat and stood beside the dead man. Lifting an edge of the sheet he pulled it away, exposing the entire body, altogether naked and showing in the candlelight a claylike yellow. It had, however, broad marks of bluish black, obviously caused by extravasated blood from contusions. The chest and sides looked as if they had been beaten with a bludgeon. There were dreadful lacerations; the skin was torn in strips and shreds.

The coroner moved round to the end of the table and undid a silk handkerchief which had been passed under the chin and knotted on the top of the head. When the handkerchief was drawn away, it exposed what had been the throat. Some of the jurors who had risen to get a better view repented their curiosity and turned away their faces. Witness Harker went to the open window and leaned across the sill, faint and sick.

Dropping the handkerchief upon the dead man's neck, the coroner stepped to a corner of the room and from a pile of clothing produced one garment after another, each of which he held up a moment for inspection. All were torn, and stiff with blood.

"Gentlemen," the coroner said, "we have no more

evidence, I think. Your duty has been already explained to you; if there is nothing you wish to ask, you may go outside and consider your verdict."

The foreman rose—a tall, bearded man of sixty. "I should like to ask one question, Mr. Coroner," he said. "What asylum did yer witness escape from?"

"Mr. Harker," said the coroner, gravely and tranquilly, "from what asylum did you last escape?"

Harker flushed crimson again but said nothing, and the seven jurors rose and solemnly filed out of the cabin.

"If you have finished insulting me, sir," said Harker, as soon as he and the officer were left alone with the dead man, "I suppose I am at liberty to go?"

"Yes."

Harker started to leave, but paused, with his hand on the door latch. The habit of his profession was strong in him—stronger than his sense of personal dignity. He turned about and said:

"The book that you have there—I recognize it as Morgan's diary. You seemed greatly interested in it; you read in it while I was testifying. May I see it? The public would like—"

"The book will cut no figure in this matter," replied the official, slipping it into his coat pocket; "all the entries in it were made before the writer's death."

As Harker passed out of the house, the jury reentered and stood about the table, on which the now covered corpse showed under the sheet with sharp definition. The foreman seated himself near the candle, produced from his breast pocket a pencil and scrap of paper, and wrote rather laboriously the following verdict, which with various degrees of effort all signed:

"We, the jury, do find that the remains come to their death at the hands of a mountain lion, but some of us thinks, all the same, they had fits."

In the diary of the late Hugh Morgan are certain interesting entries, which may possibly have some scientific value. At the inquest upon his body, the book was not put in evidence; possibly the coroner thought it not worth while to confuse the jury. The date of the first of the entries cannot be ascertained; the upper part of the leaf is torn away; the part of the entry remaining follows:

". . . would run in a half-circle, keeping his head turned always toward the center, and again he would stand still, barking furiously. At last he ran away into the brush as fast as he could go. I thought at first that he had gone mad, but on returning to the house found no other alteration in his manner than what was obviously due to fear of punishment.

"Can a dog see with his nose? Do odors impress some cerebral center with images of the thing that emitted them . . .?

Sept. 2—Looking at the stars last night, as they rose above the crest of the ridge east of the house, I observed them successively disappear—from left to right. Each was eclipsed but an instant, and only a few at the same time, but along the entire length of the ridge all that were within a degree or two of the crest were blotted out. It was as if something had passed along between me and them; but I could not see it, and the stars were not thick enough to define its outline. Ugh! I don't like this. It worries me."

Several weeks' entries are missing, three leaves being torn from the book.

"Sept. 27—It has been about here again—I find evidences of its presence every day. I watched again all last night in the same cover, gun in hand, double-charged with buckshot. In the morning the fresh footprints were there, as before. Yet I would have sworn that I did not sleep—indeed, I hardly sleep at all. It is terrible, insupportable! If these amazing experiences are real, I shall go mad; if they are fanciful, I am mad already.

"Oct. 3—I shall not go—it shall not drive me away. No, this is *my* house, *my* land. God hates a coward. . . .

"Oct. 5—I can stand it no longer; I have invited Harker to pass a few weeks with me—he has a level head. I can judge from his manner if he thinks me mad.

"Oct. 7—I have the solution of the mystery; it came to me last night—suddenly, as by revelation. How simple—how terribly simple!

"There are sounds that we cannot hear. At either end of the scale are notes that stir no chord of that imperfect instrument, the human ear. They are too high or too grave. I have observed a flock of black-birds occupying an entire tree-top—the tops of several trees—and all in full song. Suddenly—in a moment—at absolutely the same instant—all spring into the air and fly away. How? They could not all see one another—whole tree-tops intervened. At no point could a leader have been visible to all.

"There must have been a signal of warning or command, high and shrill above the din, but by me unheard. I have observed, too, the same simultaneous flight when all were silent, among not only blackbirds, but other birds—quail, for example, widely separated by bushes—even on opposite sides of a hill.

"It is known to seamen that a school of whales basking or sporting on the surface of the ocean, miles apart, with the convexity of the earth between, will sometimes dive at the same instant—all gone out of sight in a moment. The signal has been sounded—too grave for the ear of the sailor at the masthead and his comrades on the deck—who nevertheless feel its vibrations in the ship, as the stones of a cathedral are stirred by the bass of the organ.

"As with sounds, so with colors. At each end of the solar spectrum the chemist can detect the presence of what are known as 'actinic' rays. They represent colors —integral colors in the composition of light—which we are unable to discern. The human eye is an imperfect instrument; its range is but a few octaves of the real 'chromatic scale.' I am not mad; there are colors that we cannot see.

"And, God help me! the Damned Thing is of such a color!"

JOHN RUSSELL (1885-1956)

. . . *was born to a prominent American Socialist, and adopted as a Samoan chief. During his long and varied professional career, he was involved in the allied fields of journalism and publicity. Having made extensive explorations of South America, Asia, and the South Sea islands, he was frequently called upon to serve as consultant on these regions for Hollywood films.*

As a story-teller, Russell was distinctly outside the mainstream of twentieth century American fiction, favoring language and themes strongly reminiscent of Rudyard Kipling. But Russell is in no sense a mere imitator of Victorian literature, and his stories have originality and artistic merit.

"The Price of the Head" is a tale, both wry and horrifying. The singularly grisly ending is unforgettable.

THE PRICE OF THE HEAD

THE POSSESSIONS of Christopher Alexander Pellett
were these: his name, which he was always careful to
retain intact; a suit of ducks, no longer intact, in which
he lived and slept; a continuous thirst for liquor, and a
set of red whiskers. Also he had a friend. Now no man
can gain friendship, even among the gentle islands of
Polynesia, except by virtue of some quality attaching to
him. Strength, humor, villainy: he must show some
trait by which the friend can catch and hold. How,
then, explain the loving devotion lavished upon Christopher Alexander Pellett by Karaki, the company boat
boy? This was the mystery at Fufuti.

There was no harm in Pellett. He never quarreled.
He never raised his fist. Apparently he had never
learned that a white man's foot, though it wabble ever

so, is given him wherewith to kick natives out of the road. He never even cursed anyone except himself and the Chinese half-caste who sold him brandy, which was certainly allowable because the brandy was very bad.

On the other hand, there was no perceptible good in him. He had long lost the will to toil, and lately even the skill to beg. He did not smile, nor dance, nor exhibit any of the amiable eccentricities that sometimes recommend the drunken to a certain toleration. In any other part of the world he must have passed without a struggle. But some chance had drifted him to the beaches where life is as easy as a song and his particular fate had given him a friend. And so he persisted. That was all. He persisted, a sodden lump of flesh preserved in alcohol.

Karaki, his friend, was a heathen from Bougainville, where some people are smoked and others eaten. Being a black, a Melanesian, he was as much an alien in brown Fufuti as any white. He was a serious, efficient little man with deeply sunken eyes, a great mop of kinky hair, and a complete absence of expression. His tastes were simple. He wore a red cotton kerchief belted around his waist and a brass curtain ring suspended from his nose.

Some powerful chief in his home island had sold Karaki into the service of the trading company for three years, annexing his salary of tobacco and beads in advance. When the time should be accomplished, Karaki would be shipped back to Bougainville, a matter of some eight hundred miles, where he would land no richer than before except in experience. This was the custom. Karaki may have had plans of his own.

It is seldom that one of the black races of the Pacific shows any of the virtues for which subject populations are admired. Fidelity and humility can be exacted from other colors between tan and chocolate. But the black remains the inscrutable savage. His secret heart is his own. Hence the astonishment of Fufuti, which knew the ways of black recruits, when Karaki took the worthless beachcomber to his bosom.

"Hy, you, Johnny," called Moy Jack, the Chinese half-caste. "Better you come catch this fella mahster b'long you. He fella plenty too much drunk galow."

Karaki left the shade of the copra shed where he had been waiting an hour or more and came forward to receive the sagging bulk that was thrust out of doors. He took it scientifically by wrist and armpit and swung toward the beach. Moy Jack stood on his threshold watching with cynic interest.

"Hy, you," he said; "what name you make so much bobeley 'long that fella mahster? S'pose you bling me all them fella pearl; me pay you one dam fella good trade—my word!"

It annoyed Moy Jack that he had to provide the white man with a daily drunk in exchange for the little seed pearls with which Pellett was always flush. He knew where those pearls came from. Karaki did forbidden diving in the lagoon to get them. Moy Jack made a good thing of the traffic, but he could have

made a much better thing by trading directly with
Karaki for a few sticks of tobacco.

"What name you give that fella mahster all them
fella pearl?" demanded Moy Jack offensively. "He
plenty too much no good, galow. Close up he die
altogether."

Karaki did not reply. He looked at Moy Jack once,
and the half-caste trailed off into mutterings. For an
instant there showed a strange light in Karaki's dull
eyes, like the flat, green flicker of a turning shark
glimpsed ten fathoms down.

Karaki bore his charge down to the beach to the little
thatched shelter of pandanus leaves that was all his
home. Tenderly he eased Pellett to a mat, pillowed his
head, bathed him with cool water, brushed the filth
from his hair and whiskers. Pellett's whiskers were true
whiskers, the kind that sprout like the barbels of a
catfish, and they were a glorious coppery, sun-gilt red.
Karaki combed them out with a sandalwood comb.
Later he sat by with a fan and kept the flies from the
bloated face of the drunkard.

It was a little past midday when something brought
him scurrying into the open. For weeks he had been
studying every weather sign. He knew that the change
was due when the southeast trade begins to harden
through this flawed belt of calms and cross-winds. And
now, as he watched, the sharp shadows began to blur
along the sands and a film crept over the face of the
sun.

All Fufuti was asleep. The house boys snored in the

back veranda. Under his netting the agent dreamed happily of big copra shipments and bonuses. Moy Jack dozed among his bottles. Nobody would have been mad enough to stir abroad in the noon hour of repose: nobody but Karaki, the untamed black, who cared nothing for custom nor yet for dreams. The light pad of his steps was lost in the surf drone on the barrier reefs. He flitted to and fro like a wraith. And while Fufuti slept he applied himself to a job for which he had never been hired.

Karaki had long ago ascertained two vital facts: where the key to the trade-room was kept and where the rifles and ammunition were hidden. He opened the trade-room and selected three bolts of turkey red cloth, a few knives, two cases of tobacco, and a fine small axe. There was much else he might have taken as well. But Karaki was a man of simple tastes, and efficient.

With the axe he next forced the rifle chest and removed therefrom one Winchester and a big box of cartridges. With the axe again he broke into the boatsheds. Finally with the axe he smashed the bottoms out of the whale-boat and the two cutters so they would be of no use to anyone for many days to come. It was really a very handy little axe, a true tomahawk, ground to a shaving edge. Karaki took a workman's pleasure in its keen, deep strokes. It was almost his chief prize.

On the beach lay a big proa, a stout outrigger canoe of the kind Karaki's own people used at Bougainville, so high of prow and stern as to be nearly crescent-shaped. The northwest monsoon of last season had washed it ashore at Fufuti and Karaki had repaired it, by the agent's own order. This proa he now launched in the lagoon, and aboard it he stored his loot.

Of supplies he had to make a hasty selection. He took a bag of rice and another of sweet potatoes. He took as many coconuts as he could carry in a net in three trips. He took a cask of water and a box of biscuit. And here happened an odd thing.

In his search for the biscuit he came upon the agent's private store of liquor, a dozen bottles of rare Irish whisky. He glanced at them and passed them by. He knew what the stuff was, and he was a savage, a black man. But he passed it by. When Moy Jack heard of that later he remembered what he had seen in Karaki's eyes and ventured the surprising prediction that Karaki would never be taken alive.

When all was ready Karaki went back to his thatch and aroused Christopher Alexander Pellett.

"Hy, mahster, you come 'long me."

Mr. Pellett sat up and looked at him. That is to say, he looked. Whether he saw anything or not belongs among the obscurer questions of psychopathy.

"Too late," said Mr. Pellett profoundly. "This shop is closed. Copy boy! Give all those damned loafers good night. I'm—I'm goin'—bed!"

Whereupon he fell flat on his back.

"Wake up, mahster," insisted Karaki, shaking him. "You too much strong fella sleep. Hy-ah, mahster!

Rum! You like'm rum? You catch'm rum any amount —my word! Plenty rum, mahster!"

But even this magic call, which never failed to rouse Pellett from his couch in the mornings, fell now on deaf ears. Pellett had had his skinful, and the fitness of things decreed that he should soak the clock around.

Karaki knelt beside him, pried him up until he could get a shoulder under his middle, and lifted him like a loose bag of meal. Pellett weighed one hundred and fifty pounds; Karaki not much more than a hundred. Yet in some deft coolie fashion of his own the little black man packed his burden, with the feet dragging behind, clear down to the beach. Moreover, he managed to get it aboard the proa. Pellett was half drowned and the proa half swamped. But Karaki managed.

No man saw their departure. Fufuti still dreamed on. Long before the agent awoke to wrath and ruin their queer crescent craft had slipped from the lagoon and faded away on the wings of the trade.

The first day Karaki had all he could do to keep the proa running straight before the wind. Big smoky seas came piling up out of the southeast and would have piled aboard if he had given them the least chance. He was only a heathen who did not know a compass from a degree of latitude. But his forefathers used to people these waters on cockleshell voyages that made the venture of Columbus look like a ride in a ferryboat. Karaki bailed with a tin pan and sailed with a mat and steered with a paddle: but he proceeded.

Along about sunrise Mr. Pellett stirred in the bilge and raised a pea-green face. He took one bewildered glance overside at the seething waste and collapsed with a groan. After a decent interval he tried again, but this was an illusion that would not pass, and he twisted around to Karaki sitting crouched and all aglisten with spray in the stern.

"Rum!" he demanded.

Karaki shook his head, and a haunted look crept into Pellett's eyes.

"Take—take away all that stuff," he begged pathetically, pointing at the ocean.

Thereafter for two days he was very, very sick, and he learned how a small boat in any kind of a sea can move forty-seven different ways within one and the same minute. This was no trifling bit of knowledge, as those who have acquired it can tell. It was nearly fatal to Pellett.

On the third day he awoke with a mouth and a stomach of fumed leather and a great weakness, but otherwise in command of his few faculties. The gale had fallen and Karaki was quietly preparing fresh coconuts. Pellett quaffed two before he thought to miss the brandy with which his breakfast draught was always laced. But when he remembered, the milk choked in his throat.

"Me like'm rum."

"No got'm rum."

Pellett looked forward and aft, to windward and to lee. There was a great deal of horizon in sight, but nothing else. For the first time he was aware of a strangeness in events.

"What name you come so far?" he asked.

"We catch'm one big fella wind," explained Karaki.

Pellett was in no condition to question his statement nor to observe from the careful stocking of the proa that they had not been blown to sea on a casual fishing trip. Pellett had other things to think of. Some of the things were pink and others purple and others were striped like the rainbow in most surprising designs, and all were highly novel and interesting. They came thronging up out of the vasty deep to entertain Christopher Alexander Pellett. Which they did.

You cannot cut off alcohol from a man who has been continuously pickled for two years without results more or less picturesque. These were days when the proa went shouting across the empty southern seas to madrigal and choric song. Tied hand and foot and lashed under a thwart, Pellett raved in the numbers of his innocent youth. It would have been singular hearing had there been any to hear, but there was only Karaki, who did not care for the lesser Cavalier poets and on whom whole pages of "Atalanta in Calydon" were quite wasted. Now and then he threw a dipperful of seawater over the white man, or spread a mat to keep the sun from him, or fed him with coconut milk by force. Karaki was a poor audience, but an excellent nurse. Also, he combed Pellett's whiskers twice every day.

They ran into calms. But the trade picked them up

again more gently, so that Karaki ventured to make westing, and they fled under skies as bright as polished brass.

> *"My heart is within me*
> *As an ash in the fire;*
> *Whosoever hath seen me*
> *Without lute, without lyre,*
> *Shall sing of me grievous things,*
> *even things that were ill*
> *to desire—"*

Thus chanted Christopher Alexander Pellett, whose face began to show a little more like flesh and a little less like rotten kelp.

Whenever a fair chance offered, Karaki landed on the lee of some one of the tiny islets with which the Santa Cruz region is peppered, and would make shift to cook rice and potatoes in the tin dipper. This was risky, for one day the islet proved to be inhabited. Two white men in a cutter came out to stop them. Karaki could not hide his resemblance to a runaway native, and he did not try to. But when the cutter approached within fifty yards he suddenly announced himself as a runaway native with a gun. He left the cutter sinking and one of the men dead.

"There's a bullet hole alongside me here," said Pellett from under the thwart. "You'd better plug it."

Karaki plugged it and released his passenger, who sat up and began stretching himself with a certain naive curiosity of his own body.

"So you're real," observed Pellett, staring hard at Karaki. "By George, you *are,* and that's comfort."

He was right. Karaki was very real.

"What side you take'm this fella canoe?"

"Balbi," said Karaki, using the native word for Bougainville.

Pellett whistled. An eight-hundred-mile evasion in an open boat was a considerable undertaking. It enlisted his respect. Moreover, he had just had emphatic proof of the efficiency of this little black man.

"Balbi all some home b'long you?"

"Yes."

"All right, commodore," said Pellett. "Lead on. I don't know why you shipped me for supercargo, but I'll see you through."

Strangely—or perhaps not so strangely—the whole Fufuti interval of his history had been fading from his brain while the poison was ebbing from his tissues. The Christopher Alexander Pellett that emerged was one from earlier years: pretty much of a wreck, it was true, and a feckless, indolent, paltry creature at best, but ordinarily human and rather more than ordinarily intelligent.

He was very feeble at first, but Karaki's diet of coconuts and sweet potatoes did wonders for him, and the time came when he could rejoice in the good salt taste of the spray on his lips and forget for hours together the crazy craving for stimulant. They made a strange crew, this pair—simple savage and convalescent drunkard—but there was never any question as to which was in command. That was well seen in the third week when their food began to fail and Pellett noticed that Karaki ate nothing for a whole day.

"See here, this won't do," he cried. "You've given me the last coconut and kept none for yourself."

"Me no like'm eat," said Karaki shortly.

Christopher Alexander Pellett pondered many matters in long, idle hours while the rush of foam under the proa and the creak and fling of her outriggers were the only sounds between sea and sky. Sometimes his brow was knotted with pain. It is not always pleasant to be wrenched back into level contact with one's memories. Thoughts are no sweeter company for having long been drowned. He had met the horrors of delirium. He had now to face the livelier devils of his past. He had fled them before.

But here was no escape of any kind. So he turned and grappled with them and laid them one by one.

When they had been at sea twenty-nine days they had nothing left of their provisions but a little water. Karaki doled it out by moistening a shred of coconut husk and giving Pellett the shred to suck. In spite of Pellett's petulant protest, he would take none himself. Again the heathen nursed the derelict, this time through the last stages of thirst, scraping the staves of the cask and feeding him the ultimate drop of moisture on the point of a knife.

On the thirty-sixth day from Fufuti they sighted Choiseul, a great green wall that built up slowly across the west. Karaki steered directly towards the green island.

Once fairly under its headlands, Karaki might have indulged a certain triumph. He had taken as his target the whole length of the Solomons, some six hundred miles. But to have fetched the broadside of them any-where in such a craft as the proa through storm and current, without instrument or chart, was distinctly a feat of navigation. Karaki, however, did no celebrating. Instead, he stared long and anxiously over his shoulder into the east.

The wind had been fitful since morning. By noon it was dead calm on a restless, oily sea. A barometer would have told evil tales, but Karaki must have guessed them anyway, for he staggered forward and unstepped the little mast. Then he bound all his cargo securely under the thwarts and put all his remaining strength into the paddle, heading for a small outpost island where a line of white showed beach. They had been very lucky thus far, but they were still two miles offshore when the first rush of the hurricane caught them.

Karaki himself was reduced to a rattle of bones in a dried skin, and Pellett could scarce lift a hand. But Karaki fought for Pellett among the waves that leaped up like sheets of fire on the reef. Why or how they got through neither could have said. Perhaps because it was written that after drink, illness, madness, and starvation the white man should be saved by the black man again and a last time from ravening waters. When they came ashore on the islet they were both nearly flayed, but they were alive, and Karaki still gripped

Pellett's shirt. They fell down together in exhaustion.

For a week they stayed while Pellett fattened on un-limited coconut and Karaki tinkered the proa. It had landed in a water-logged tangle, but Karaki's treasures were safe. He got his bearings from a passing native fisherman, and then he knew that *all* his treasures were safe. His home island lay across Bougainville Strait, the stretch of water just beyond.

"Balbi over there?" asked Pellett.

"Yes," said Karaki.

"And a mighty good thing too," cried Pellett heart-ily. "This is the limit of British authority, old boy. Big fella mahster b'long Beretani stop'm here, no can go that side."

Karaki was quite aware of it. If he feared one thing in the world, he feared the Fiji High Court and its Resident Commissioner for the Southern Solomons, who did sure justice upon all who transgressed in its jurisdiction. Once beyond the strait he might still be liable for the stolen goods and the broken contract. But never—this was the point—never could he be punished for anything he might choose to do over there in Bougainville.

So Karaki was content.

And so was Christopher Alexander Pellett. His body had been wrung and swept and scoured, and he had downed his devils. Sweet air and sunshine were on his lips and in his heart. His bones were sweet in him. As his vigor returned he swam the lagoon or helped Karaki at the proa. He would spend hours hugging the warm sand or rejoicing in the delicate tracery of some tiny sea-shell, singing softly to himself, while the ground-swell hushed along the beach, savoring life as he never had done.

"Oh, this is good—good!" he said.

Karaki puzzled him. Not that he vexed himself, for a smiling wonder at anything, almost childlike, filled him these days. But he thought of this taciturn savage, how he had capped thankless service with rarest sacrifice. And now that he could consider soberly, the why of it eluded him. Why? Affection? Friendship? It must be so, and he warmed toward the silent little man with the sunken eyes and the expressionless face from which he could never raise a wink.

"Hy, you, Karaki, what name you no laugh all same me? What? You too much fright 'long that fella stuff you steal? Forget it, you old black scamp. If they ever trouble you, I'll square them somehow. By George, I'll say I stole it myself!"

Karaki only grunted and sat down to clean his Winchester with a bit of rag and some drops of oil he had crushed from a dried coconut.

"No, that don't reach him either," murmured Pellett, baffled. "I'd like to know what's going on under that topknot of yours, old chap. You're like Kipling's cat, that walks by himself. God knows I'm not ungrateful. I wish I could show you—"

He sprang up.

"Karaki! Me one big fella friend 'long you: savee? You one big fella friend 'long me: savee? We two dam' big fella friend, my word! . . . What?"

"Yes," said Karaki. No other response. He looked at Pellett and he looked away toward Bougainville. "Yes," he said, "my word," and went on cleaning his gun—the black islander, inscrutable, incomprehensible, an enigma always, and to the end.

The end came two days later at Bougainville.

Under a gorgeous dawn they came into a bay that opened before their prow as with jeweled arms of welcome. The land lay lapped in bright garments like a sleeper half awakened, all flushed and smiling, sensuous, intimate, thrilling with life, breathing warm scents—

These were some of the foolish phrases Pellett babbled to himself as he leaped ashore and ran up on a rocky point to see and to feel and to draw all the charm of the place to himself.

Meanwhile Karaki, that simple and efficient little man, was proceeding methodically about his own affairs. He landed his bolts of cloth, his tobacco, his knives, and the other loot. He landed his box of cartridges and his rifle and his fine tomahawk. The goods were somewhat damaged by sea water, but the weapons had been carefully cleaned and polished.

Pellett was declaiming poetry aloud to the alluring solitude when he was aware of a gentle footfall and turned, surprised, to find Karaki standing just behind him with the rifle at his hip and the axe in his hand.

"Well," said Pellett cheerfully, "what d'you want, old chappie?"

"Me like," said Karaki, while there gleamed in his eyes the strange light that Moy Jack had glimpsed there, like the flicker of a turning shark; "me like'm too much one fella head b'long you!"

"What? Head! Whose—my head?"

"Yes," said Karaki simply.

That was the way of it. That was all the mystery. The savage had fallen enamored of the head of the beachcomber, and Christopher Alexander Pellett had been betrayed by his fatal red whiskers. In Karaki's country a white man's head, well smoked, is a thing to be desired above wealth, above lands and chiefship's fame, and the love of women. In all Karaki's country was no head like the head of Pellett. Therefore Karaki had served to win it with the patience and single faith of a Jacob. For this he had schemed and waited, committed theft and murder, expended sweat and cunning, starved and denied himself, nursed, watched, tended, fed, and saved his man that he might bring the head alive and on the hoof—so to speak—to the spot where he could remove it at leisure and enjoy the fruits of his labor in safety.

Pellett saw all this at a flash, understood it so far as any white could understand it: the whole elemental and stupendous simplicity of it. And standing there in his new strength and sanity under the fair promise of the morning, he gave a laugh that pealed across the waters and started the birds from their cliffs, the deep-throated laugh of a man who fathoms and accepts the last great jest. He laughed at the bitter irony of it all.

For finally, by corrected list, the possessions of Christopher Alexander Pellett were these: his name still intact; the ruins of some rusty ducks; his precious red whiskers—and a soul which had been neatly recovered, renewed, refurbished, reanimated, and restored to him by his good friend Karaki.

> *"Thou shouldst die as he dies,*
>   *For whom none sheddeth tears;*
> *Filling thine eyes*
>   *And fulfilling thine ears*
> *With the brilliance . . . the bloom*
>   *and the beauty . . ."*

Thus chanted Christopher Alexander Pellett over the waters of the bay, and then whirled, throwing wide his arms:

"Shoot, damn you! It's cheap at the price!"

FREDRIC BROWN *(1906-   )*

. . . was born in Cincinnati and now lives in the southwest. He has written some three hundred short stories and 29 novels, mostly mysteries and works of science fiction. He is married and has two children. The typical Fredric Brown story has two chief characteristics: it is short, and it packs the reader a really brutal wallop. "Granny's Birthday" may be one of the shortest stories in this collection; it is undoubtedly also one of the most devastating.

GRANNY'S BIRTHDAY

—not even murder!

THE HALPERINS were a very close-knit family. Wade Smith, one of the only two non-Halperins present, envied them that, since he had no family himself—but the envy was tempered into a mellow glow by the glass in his hand.

It was Granny Halperin's birthday party, her eightieth birthday; everyone present except Smith and one other man was a Halperin, and was named Halperin. Granny had three sons and a daughter; all were present and the three sons were married and had their wives with them. That made eight Halperins, counting Granny. And there were four members of the second generation, grandchildren, one with his wife, and that made thirteen Halperins. Thirteen Halperins, Smith counted; with himself and the other non-Halperin, a man named Cross, that made fifteen adults. And there had been, earlier, three more Halperins, great-grandchildren, but they had been put to bed earlier in the evening, at various hours according to their respective ages.

And he liked them all, Smith thought mellowly, although now that the children had been abed a while, liquor was flowing freely and the party was getting a bit loud and boisterous for his taste. Everyone was drinking; even Granny, seated on a chair not unlike a throne, had a glass of sherry in her hand, her third for the evening.

She was a wonderfully sweet and vivacious little old lady, Smith thought. Definitely, though, a matriarch; sweet as she was, Smith was thinking; she ruled her family with a rod of iron in a velvet glove; he was just inebriated enough to get his metaphors mixed.

He, Smith, was here because he'd been invited by Bill Halperin, who was one of Granny's sons; he was Bill's attorney and also his friend. The other outsider, a Gene or Jean Cross, seemed to be a friend of several of the grandson-generation Halperins.

Across the room he saw that Cross was talking to Hank Halperin and noticed that whatever they were saying had suddenly led to raised and angry voices. Smith hoped there wouldn't be trouble; the party was much too pleasant to be broken up now by a fight or even an argument.

But suddenly Hank Halperin's fist lashed out and

caught Cross's jaw and Cross went backward and fell. His head hit on the stone edge of the fireplace with a loud *thunk* and he lay still. Hank quickly ran, knelt beside Cross and touched him, and then Hank was pale as he looked up and then stood up. "Dead," he said said thickly. "God, I didn't mean to—But he said—"

Granny wasn't smiling now. Her voice rose sharp and querulously. "He tried to hit you first, Henry. *I* saw it. We *all* saw it, didn't we?"

She had turned, with the last sentence, to frown at Wade Smith, the surviving outsider.

Smith moved uncomfortably. "I—I didn't see the start of it, Mrs. Halperin."

"You did," she snapped. "You were looking right at them, Mr. Smith."

Before Wade Smith could answer, Hank Halperin was saying, "Lord, Granny, I'm sorry—but even that's no answer. This is *real* trouble. Remember I fought seven years in the ring as a pro. And the fists of a boxer or an ex-boxer are legally considered lethal weapons. That makes it second-degree murder even if he did hit first. You know that, Mr. Smith; you're a lawyer. And with the other trouble I've been in, the cops will throw the book at me."

"I—I'm afraid you're probably right," Smith said uneasily. "But hadn't somebody better phone a doctor or the police, or both?"

"In a minute, Smith," Bill Halperin, Smith's friend, said. "We got to get this straightened out among ourselves first. It *was* self-defense, wasn't it?"

"I—I guess. I don't know what to—"

"Wait, everybody," Granny's sharp voice cut in. "Even if it was self-defense, Henry's in trouble. And do you think we can *trust* this man Smith once he's out of here and in court?"

Bill Halperin said, "But, Granny, we'll *have* to—"

"Nonsense, William. *I* saw what happened. We all did. They got in a fight, Cross and Smith, and killed each other. Cross killed Smith and then, dizzy from the blows he'd taken himself, fell and hit his head. We're not going to let Henry go to jail, are we, children? Not a Halperin, not *one of us*. Henry, muss that body up a little, so it'll look like he was in a fight, not just a one-punch business. And the rest of you—"

The male Halperins, except Henry, were in a circle around Smith now; the women, except Granny, were right behind them—and the circle closed in.

The last thing Smith saw clearly was Granny in her throne-like chair, her eyes beady with excitement and determination. And the last thing Smith heard in the sudden silence which he could no longer make his voice penetrate was the soft sound of Granny Halperin's chuckling. Then the first blow rocked him.

H. VERNOR DIXON (1908-   )

. . . has had an unusually diversified career. He first earned his living as an actor in a highly successful brother-and-sister vaudeville team, even appearing in a few movies. However, Dixon never really liked show business, and was actually relieved when vaudeville folded in the early 1930's. He then tried his hand at fiction writing, and proved very successful in this field, too. Avocationally, he is a sometime inventor, and he has been an amateur airplane pilot since his teens. During the 1940's, he contributed significantly to the development of the Landgraf Helicopter.

In "Trapped," Dixon tellingly combines his knowledge of technology with his craft as a writer. You will not easily forget this gripping—and mechanically accurate—account of an agonizing journey through an underground drainage system.

TRAPPED!

—beneath a flaming warehouse

with no way out!

JOHN WAS READY to leave his office when he noticed a memo on his desk reading: "Silverware. Crane's Warehouse." It was his wife's handwriting. Ellen must have come in while he was out and left the cryptic message. John had to smile. Ellen's assumption that he would know what she meant was so typical.

The silverware had been left to him by an elderly aunt, recently deceased. Some of it was extremely valuable, but Ellen had said it was in odd pieces and unmatched units so that it could not be used at home and they might just as well sell it.

He wondered if "Crane's Warehouse" meant that Ellen had been to the storage vaults to look it over, have it transported home, or appraised, or if she wanted him to do something about it. He wondered just what she meant.

Then he had too many other important matters on his mind. Only that day the city commissioners had informed him that he had been awarded the contracts for the new sewage and outfall systems and the three-million-dollar disposal plant. Every architect and contractor in the state had been after those contracts, and John had won out. Now he had an opportunity to live up to the reputation of the business he had inherited from Ellen's father. The old contractor had been a big man in the state. When he died suddenly and John took over, he'd expected the business to go on as usual. But it had not worked out that way. John had to prove himself. Well, he'd done it now. These contracts meant he was accepted at the top. Ellen would be delighted when she heard the news.

It was dusk when he walked out to the street and headed for the parking lot. At thirty-nine he was a tall, rather broad-shouldered man whom life and the years had treated kindly. His dark brown hair was beginning to turn gray at the temples, but his eyes were clear. A twice-weekly workout at the Athletic Club helped to keep him fit. He believed firmly that a man should keep in shape. But, on the other hand, it had never crossed his mind that his life would one day depend on it.

When he reached his car he started automatically for home. At the first red light, however, he changed his mind. Jimmy was having football practice at high school, which would mean a late dinner. He could drive to Crane's where the silver was stored, and learn if Ellen had made any arrangements.

Crane's was the largest single structure in town. The huge warehouse of brick, cement and old wood occupied an entire square block and spilled over into offices along a side street. The barred windows were all dark. John turned around the corner of the warehouse to the offices, but they were also dark.

He was about to drive away when he saw a man shuffle across the street and unlock a door of the warehouse. John quickly parked the car and hurried to intercept the man, who turned out to be Sam Moran, the night watchman. John had used him on contracting jobs and though he had had to fire him for drinking on the job he still liked the old man.

John explained what he was after, and Moran thought he could at least find out if the silver had been moved. As customers sometimes telephoned after hours, receipts were always left in the watchman's office for goods moved that day.

John followed him into the gloomy warehouse and along a dark corridor that bisected the building. They passed through a heavy door into a tiny room cluttered with baled papers, magazines, some broken chairs, a roll-top desk and a blanket-covered Army cot. The room was overly warm and smelled from the fumes of a smoking kerosene stove.

Moran hung his heavy mackinaw on a hook beside the stove. John thought it was dangerously close to the stove, but his attention was diverted by Moran snapping open the desk and going through a pile of papers. He nodded after a moment, held a piece of paper and said, "Yep, she's been here. Didn't move the stuff, though. Just had it appraised and insured for forty thousand."

A smile tugged at the corners of John's lips. Then the memo on the desk had been simply to let him know that everything was taken care of. That was so like Ellen. The two had such a close affinity that she expected him to guess everything from a few words. A feeling of warmth stole through John that had nothing to do with the atmosphere of the room.

Moran squinted at John. "Y'know," he said, "I'm willin' to let bygones be bygones if you are."

"How do you mean?"

"Don't you remember givin' me the bounce for takin' a drink now and then?"

"Oh," John laughed. "I've never held that against you. You can always come back with me if you ever want to."

"That's mighty nice of you. What say we have a drink on it? I got a nice bottle stashed away down below," Moran said. "How about it, Mr. Mead?"

"I don't know—"

"Now, look, lad, a little one never hurt anybody. Make it a toast to old times."

John didn't want to appear stuffy. "Well," he laughed, "since you're twisting my arm—"

He followed Moran down a long flight of stairs. At the bottom there was a damp concrete wall, with a small steel door about the size and shape of bulkhead doors in submarines. Moran swung it open and stepped into black darkness. John followed him through as soon as a light was turned on. Moran closed the steel door behind them.

John looked curiously about the small room in which he found himself. It was built of solid concrete —walls, floor and ceiling—about eight feet high and twenty feet square. There were some boxes in one corner of the room, some steel filing cabinets and, in the center of the floor, an old kitchen table and two chairs. Embedded in two of the walls were disconnected pipes, broken gauges, rusted dials and valve handles. There was no other entrance to the room except the one they had used. The single source of light was from a battery-type lantern hanging from a valve in the ceiling.

The watchman swung one of the broken pipes around to extract two glasses and a bottle of bourbon. As he placed them on the table he noticed John's eyes traveling about the room. He explained, "This place has been all kinds of things; a control room for furnaces, a bank vault and even a water reservoir. It ain't used for nothin' now."

He poured two husky slugs of whisky into the glasses and shoved one of them across the table to John. The watchman sighed with satisfaction as the whisky warmed his throat, and began talking about old times in the contracting game.

John was anxious to leave. The room gave him a ghostly feeling of unease. But he wanted to be polite, so he sat down and listened to Moran's tales. In spite of his anxiety, he became interested in Moran's reminiscences and injected some stories of his own. They had another drink, talked a few minutes longer, and then John got up to leave.

Moran placed the bottle and glasses back in the pipe and slapped John's shoulder as he passed him to move toward the closed door. As he placed his hand on the steel handle a puzzled expression crept into his eyes. He stared at the door for a moment. Then slowly he raised his hand and placed it flat against the steel. His bushy eyebrows came together in a worried frown.

John stepped forward and placed his own hand on the door. "The steel seems to be warm."

"Yeah."

They looked into each other's eyes for a split second and hastily away. John felt suddenly weak and limp, but he pushed the watchman aside, grasped the steel handle and shoved the door open. The silence of the vault was instantly shattered by an enormous, ear-splitting roar, as if a thousand explosions were taking place simultaneously. Vicious heat battered at them.

The stairway at the end of the corridor had disappeared in a burst of flame, and the corridor itself was a river of fire, sparks, embers and burning beams falling from the floor above. John stepped back, slammed the door closed and was again in the silence of a tomb.

For a moment, John felt that he was going to faint. He leaned weakly against the concrete wall and looked at Moran, who was staring vacantly at the door. John whispered, "That heater started it."

Moran nodded, then turned his head to blink at John. "Man, the whole warehouse is on fire! We're *trapped.*"

John closed his eyes and considered the central location of the watchman's dingy office. The fire would spread from there in all directions, racing across the ground floor and then leaping upward to the other floors. The block-square building was eight stories high, each floor jammed with furniture, perishable goods and tons of combustible items.

There was some concrete and steel in the structure, but the building was old and consisted principally of wood. The fire was probably out of control at the moment it started. Fire trucks must be screaming into the adjoining streets, but John knew with terrible certainty that a fire in that building could never be put out until it had collapsed and burnt itself out.

Collapsed over our heads, he thought.

He felt the concrete getting warm against his shoulder and moved away. He placed his hand on the steel door and quickly withdrew it. The door was now actually hot. He looked frantically about the room, searching wildly for a means of escape. There was no other exit. He glanced at the light, which had been left on, and noticed it swaying slightly on the valve. Timbers were probably already crashing against the concrete ceiling. He wondered about its thickness and if it would hold.

The watchman followed the direction of his eyes

and gasped, "It's solid. All concrete and steel. Maybe four feet thick. I don't think it will break."

"How about the walls?"

"Same thickness."

A wave of nausea swept through John, and then his weakness drained away. He walked slowly about the four walls of the room, examining the broken pipes. None of them seemed to pierce the walls. They were probably filled with concrete. At least, fire and smoke would not be able to get through. But where, he wondered, was air coming from? There was not a single vent in the walls or ceiling.

He searched the room and under the table found a large manhole in the floor. He got down to his knees and sniffed at the holes in the iron cover. Cool, musty air was in his nostrils. Evidently the manhole went down to a disposal pipe of some kind that was open to outside air. Otherwise he would detect heat. Thank God for that, he thought, as he got back to his feet.

Moran put his bottle and glasses back on the table and helped himself to the whisky. Then he cleared his throat and said huskily, "Ain't there nothin' we can do?"

"I can't think of anything. There's only the one exit, and we can't use that." He saw the fear growing in Moran's eyes and said quickly, "They'll probably be able to dig us out in a day or two."

"If anybody looks."

Moran screamed, "Man, there must be something!"

John did not reply. He looked down at his hands on

the table and saw that they were shaking. He tightened his hands into fists. He had to keep control of himself . . .

Don't let me go to pieces. Don't let it happen. I can hold on. I know I can hold on. Just let me hold on till it is over with and someone gets us out . . .

The air in the room was getting very warm. Beads of perspiration appeared on the faces of the two men and the backs of their hands. Moran shifted uncomfortably in the heat, offering the bottle. John shook his head and watched Moran finish the whisky. The watchman's head bobbed drunkenly on his shoulders.

The heat deepened in the room. John took off his coat and vest. In another few minutes he had taken off his tie and shirt. Perspiration was streaming from him. He was afraid to think of what was happening over him, but his brain was intent on visualizing the holocaust, the flames and smoke shooting hundreds of feet in the air, the night made hideous with the roaring of the fire, the crashing of timbers, sections of the building giving way, whole floors crashing through the pitiful efforts of midget-men directing tiny streams of water.

He thought of the great burning pile settling directly onto the vault in which he was imprisoned, and his brain came up with the parallel image of food being barbecued under clay and hot rocks. For the first time he realized that he and the watchman were actually trapped in a giant oven. They would slowly but inevitably be roasted to death even if the concrete held, which, he then knew, was not possible. Under such terrible heat the concrete would crack and explode and the vault would collapse. But long before that happened he and Moran would be roasted.

John jumped to his feet and rushed around the walls like a trapped animal. He could no longer touch the concrete. Even the metal strap of his wristwatch was becoming too hot for his skin. He took it off and dropped it on the floor. He sank back into the chair at the grimy table and blinked at the watchman, whose head was slowly sinking lower. Moran's skin was becoming a mottled red from the heat. John realized sickly that his own skin probably looked the same.

He looked at death, then, and faced it. Panic left him and the beat of his raging heart became calmer. It was human to hope, but here there was no hope. Even a man in a trapped submarine at the bottom of the ocean could hope that somehow there was a way out. But there was no hope in the vault.

There was but one single, inescapable fact—he would be roasted. A man being strapped in an electric chair had a better chance to live. No one could send a reprieve to the vault. Death filled the room.

John accepted it and turned away from it and thought of his family. Ellen and Jimmy would be secure, at least. There was the business to sell, there was ample insurance and there was the trust fund put aside for Jimmy's education. Ironically, too, the silver in the warehouse would now bring in an additional forty thousand dollars from the insurance policy. There was no worry about their future. No worry at all.

He considered the past, racing through it in his mind to savor its every moment. It had been good. He and Ellen had been in love when they married, and that love had increased and intensified through sixteen years.

They had always been very close. He thought of a favorite remark of Ellen's, "We were truly fated for each other, darling. I think Fate will always play a large part in our marriage." Then she would ask, "Don't you believe that, too?" and he would admit that he did. There had been nothing ordinary about their marriage. Perhaps he could have pushed harder for material success, but now he was just as glad that he had not. It would have taken time from Ellen.

That closeness, that feeling of oneness, was now something to be cherished beyond anything material. That was the real past and all of the pure gold of the past. Even facing death he was content with the way it had been. Life had been good to him.

When he heard a telephone ringing he thought his senses were playing tricks on him. He raised his head and, with the action, came out of the fog of heat enveloping his brain. The bell was still ringing. The sound seemed to emanate from the filing cabinets. It was true. There was a telephone working in the room.

He did not wonder why. He got groggily to his feet and shook Moran. The watchman sagged back in the chair, fell sideways and crashed to the floor. His swollen mouth was open and his eyeballs were staring at nothingness. *Was it really that bad already?*

He staggered around the table, bumped against a filing cabinet and burned the flesh of his arm. He shoved the cabinet aside and behind it on a wall bracket was the phone. John stared at it with fascination. When he lifted the phone from the cradle it burned his hand, but he hung onto it. It took him almost a full minute to wet his lips and clear his throat sufficiently to speak. "Hello?"

A voice crashed in his ear, "My God, is there really someone there?"

John repeated dully, "Hello?"

The voice became hysterical with excitement. "Hey, wait a minute. This can't be. I was just trying the lines to see how many had been burned out. Wait." There was silence for a second, then the voice said, "This can't be a trick. I know where this goes. I'm connected to the vault under the warehouse."

John swallowed hard and said, "That's right. That's where I am."

"You're down there under that fire?"

"Yes. Trapped. The watchman—I—Who is this?"

"Devlin, manager of Crane's. I'm in the main office. This line we're talking on goes down under the vault and across the street. That's why it's working. But I never really thought—Say, who are you?"

"John Mead."

"Not the contractor!"

"Yes. We're trapped. Roasting. We're roasting. D'you hear me?"

"Oh, God, yes. Hold on." There was another short

silence, and then Devlin again. His voice was flat, tone-less. "Anyone you care to talk to, Mead? I can cut this line in on the city switchboard."

That was it, John thought. He knows too. He said, still tonelessly, "Yes, get me Empire 2931."

John closed his eyes and waited, fighting wildly for control. After seconds that seemed years, struggling for the right casual tone, he said, "Hello, Jimmy."

"Oh, Dad. Say, where are you? Mom's been a little worried."

"Yes. I—I'm downtown, Jimmy. Do you hear me all right?"

"Sure. Why not?"

"Where is your mother?"

"She's down the street. Mrs. Overbright's. You know that book league thing they're in together. They gotta talk over—"

John interrupted quickly, "I know." There was no time to call Ellen. There was no time to get Jimmy to go after her. But talking to Jimmy was almost the same as talking with Ellen. He wet his thickening lips and said, "I only have a moment, Jimmy."

"Something you want, Dad? Say, what do you think of that fire? Isn't that a beauty?"

John asked dully, "Crane's?"

"Sure. Even way out here the whole sky is all lit up. Boy, oh boy, what a sight. I wanted to go down and watch it, but Mom—"

John cried, "No, Jimmy, *no*. You stay home. Do you hear me?"

"Well, sure—but, gee—gee—I thought I'd—"

"Look, Jimmy, I just called to say—well—tell your mother—" He paused. What was there to say?

"Yes, Dad?"

"Nothing, Jimmy."

"Say, you sound kind of funny."

He had to hang up. He could not go on. "Good-by, Jimmy. I—I'll be seeing you."

"Sure. Good-by, Dad."

He dropped the phone back in the cradle and then thought of the thousands of things he could have said and was just as glad that they remained unsaid.

He staggered away from the filing cabinet and dropped to his knees by Moran's side. The room was now indeed an oven. Every breath was a searing pain in his lungs. He placed a hand on the watchman's chest and felt nothing. He reached for his wrist and felt the pulse. Moran was dead. He started to stretch out at his side. The phone was ringing again. John crawled across the floor, fought his way to his feet and lifted the phone. "Yes?"

"Mead. Devlin here." He sounded breathless, excited. "You hear me, Mead?"

"Yes."

"There may be a chance. There is no way to get at you. We can't do it. I've been talking with the fire chief. It's hopeless. We can hardly stand the heat even here in the offices. But there may be a chance. Isn't there a manhole there in the middle of that vault?"

"Yes."

"Thank God, it hasn't been plugged. Listen closely. That's the top of a twenty-inch pipe that drops down from the vault, goes under the street and comes out in back of our offices. It's part of an old abandoned drainage system built years ago.

"Now then, firemen are already knocking off the top of the pipe over here. If you can get down in there and crawl through we'll let a rope down from this end and pull you out. I don't know if it can be done. The pipe may even be filled up somewhere. But it's worth a try. You and Sam Moran—"

"The watchman is dead."

"Then get going, man. Don't waste time. Try it!"

John dropped the phone and fell again to his knees. He crawled to the center of the room and placed his hands on the manhole cover. The hot iron burnt his flesh. He pried and tore at the heavy cover, but could not budge it.

Strength. Just a little strength. Just enough strength. He pulled a chair over, broke a leg loose and pried it into the cover. It began to give. He levered the cover out of the hole and shoved it aside. He looked down into blackness.

For a moment he hesitated. He would have to go head first and he had no idea how far he would drop. Then, too, even though air did come through, the pipe was probably well filled with silt.

He thought of his words to Jimmy, "I'll be seeing you," and that decided him. Anything was worth trying, even if he went from one trap to another.

He extended his arms down into the pipe, lowered his head and shoulders and slid down until the cold iron was scraping his shoulders. He let his knees go and then was full length in the pipe and falling and his hands hit bottom. The drop had not been more than seven feet. But his arms would have buckled except for the confining diameter of the pipe.

He felt weak and helpless in the black hole and panic swept through him in waves. He wondered, amazed and astounded, how he managed to retain his sanity. He wanted to yell and scream.

When he felt a slight return of strength he shoved his hands forward and felt the curve of the pipe. His body could not bend enough to make the curve. He squirmed and wiggled and rolled to his back and bent up against the curve and then he was sliding through with his head and shoulders into the curve and his body following after. He clawed at the pipe and pulled himself into the flat horizontal part and rolled over again to his stomach.

He lay there in blackness and reeking mud and forgot his lacerated shoulders in the grateful coolness of the iron and the mud. He lay there for a long while, and then his arms went slowly forward into the silt. It was not very deep, about five or six inches. He squirmed into the ooze and inched forward with elbows and knees, crawling at snail's pace.

Slowly, inch by painful inch, he traveled forward through the pipe, trying to reckon his progress and the probable length of the pipe. He knew he had to travel at least two hundred yards, and that logically it could not be done.

He discarded logic and thought only of the inches. Another two or three inches; another, another. He went forward.

Time had no meaning. Even pain ceased to exist. There was but one elemental fact left in the world and that was movement, squirming, wiggling, forward movement. It went on for years and ages and space in time, but it went on. And at the end he felt another upcurve of the pipe and dug his way through deeper silt and rolled again to his back so that his stomach would fit around the curve and shoved himself forward and up.

He heard voices far above echoing in the pipe and then he felt the dangling rope and with all that was left he fought to pull the rope down and smeared it with the blood of his hands as he tied it in a firm knot around his chest and felt himself being lifted, *lifted...*

He was conscious of being pulled from the pipe and into the open air below a red and black night and of crowds milling around and shouting and talking and the stretcher and then the ambulance. He could hear the siren and felt the movement of the ambulance and the rush of its progress over the streets. But he felt something deeper, closer, tender and embracing, a part of himself, and knew that Ellen was near.

He forced his eyes open. Ellen was kneeling on the floor of the ambulance, an arm about his head, looking down into his eyes. She was pale, and her eyes were wide, but not with fear. He knew what she would say

She placed a cool cheek against his and whispered, "John."

"Yes."

"I always said—about us—"

"I know. It's true."

"More than either of us realized, my darling. Years ago—when he was contracting—it was my father who built that pipe."

John relaxed. I guess, he thought, I should have known. He smiled and closed his eyes.

MAX BRAND

. . . was one of the pen names used by Frederick Shiller Faust, one of the most remarkable and prolific American writers of our time. He is credited with at least 115 published books and over 350 magazine serials and novelettes. While he is best known for his stories and novels of the Old West, Faust's first love was poetry, and he published two volumes of verse under his own name. His popularity extended beyond America, and his works have been translated into countless foreign languages.

In 1944, on assignment for Harper's *with the Fifth Army in Italy, he accompanied an infantry unit leading the attack on a German-held position. He was killed in the first half-hour of the assault and buried in a soldier's grave.*

The skill and economy with which Max Brand evoked mood, atmosphere and character, the suspense and dramatic tension with which he built his stories are revealed perfectly in "Wine on the Desert."

WINE ON THE DESERT

proved to be a bitter draught

THERE WAS no hurry, except for the thirst, like clotted salt in the back of his throat, and Durante rode on slowly, rather enjoying the last moments of dryness before he reached the cold water in Tony's house. There was really no hurry at all. He had almost twenty-four hours head start, for they would not find his dead man until this morning. After that, there would be perhaps several hours of delay before the sheriff gathered a sufficient posse and started on his trail. Or perhaps the sheriff would be fool enough to come alone.

Durante had been able to see the wheel and fan of Tony's windmill for more than an hour, but he could not make out the ten acres of the vineyard until he had topped the last rise, for the vines had been planted in a hollow. The lowness of the ground, Tony used to say, accounted for the water that gathered in the well during the wet season. The rains sank through the desert sand, through the gravels beneath, and gathered in a bowl of clay hardpan far below.

In the middle of the rainless season the well ran dry, but long before that Tony had every drop of the water pumped up into a score of tanks made of cheap corrugated iron. Slender pipe lines carried the water from the tanks to the vines, and from time to time let them sip enough life to keep them, until the winter sky darkened overhead suddenly, one November day, and the rain came down, and all the earth made a great hushing sound as it drank. Durante had heard that whisper of drinking when he was here before; but he had never seen the place in the middle of the long drought.

The windmill looked like a sacred emblem to Durante, and the twenty stodgy, tar-painted tanks blessed his eyes; but a heavy sweat broke out at once from his body. For the air of the hollow, unstirred by wind, was hot and still as a bowl of soup, a reddish soup. The vines were powdered with thin red dust, also. They were wretched, dying things to look at; for the grapes had been gathered; the new wine had been made, and now the leaves hung in ragged tatters.

Durante rode up to the squat adobe house, and right through the entrance into the patio. A flowering vine clothed three sides of the little court. Durante did not know the name of the plant, but it had large white blossoms with golden hearts that poured sweetness on the air. Durante hated the sweetness. It made him more thirsty.

He threw the reins of his mule and strode into the house. The water cooler stood in the hall outside the kitchen. There were two jars made of a porous stone, very ancient things, and the liquid which distilled through the pores kept the contents cool. The jar on the left held water; that on the right contained wine. There was a big tin dipper hanging on a peg beside each jar. Durante tossed off the cover of the vase on the left and plunged the dipper in until the delicious coolness closed well above his wrist.

"Hey, Tony," he called. Out of his dusty throat the cry was a mere groaning. He drank and called again, clearly, "Tony!"

A voice pealed from the distance.

Durante, pouring down the second dipper of water, smelled the alkali dust which had shaken off his own clothes. It seemed to him that heat was radiating like light from his clothes, from his body; and the cool dimness of the house was soaking it up. He heard Tony's wooden leg bumping on the ground, and Durante grinned; then in came Tony, with that hitch and side-swing with which he accommodated the stiffness of his artificial leg. His brown face shone with sweat as though a special ray of light were focused on it.

"Ah, Dick!" he said. "Good old Dick! . . . How long

since you came last! . . . Wouldn't Julia be glad! Wouldn't she be glad?"

"Ain't she here?" asked Durante, jerking his head suddenly away from the dripping dipper.

"She's away at Nogalez," said Tony. "It gets so hot. I said, 'You go up to Nogalez, Julia, where the wind don't forget to blow.' She cried, but I made her go."

"Did she cry?" asked Durante.

"Julia . . . that's a good girl," said Tony.

"Yeah. You bet she's good," said Durante. He put the dipper quickly to his lips, but did not swallow for a moment; he was grinning too widely. Afterward he said, "You wouldn't throw some water into that mule of mine, would you, Tony?"

Tony went out with his wooden leg clumping loudly on the wooden floor, softly in the patio dust. Durante found the hammock in the corner of the patio. He lay down in it and watched the colors of sunset flush the mists of desert dust that rose to the zenith. The water was soaking through his body; hunger began, and then the rattling of pans in the kitchen and the cheerful cry of Tony's voice:

"What you want, Dick? I got some pork. You don't want pork. I'll make you some good Mexican beans. Hot. Ah, ha! I know that old Dick. I have plenty of good wine for you, Dick. And tortillas. Even Julia can't make tortillas like me. — And what about a nice young rabbit?"

"All blowed full of buckshot?" growled Durante.

"No, no. I kill them with the rifle."

"You kill rabbits with a rifle?" repeated Durante, with a quick interest.

"It's the only gun I have," said Tony. "If I catch them in the sight, they are dead.—A wooden leg cannot walk very far — I must kill them quick, you see? They come close to the house about sunrise and flop their ears. I shoot through the head."

"Yeah? Yeah?" muttered Durante. "Through the head?" He relaxed, scowling. He passed his hand over his face, over his head.

Then Tony began to bring the food out into the patio and lay it on a small wooden table. A lantern hanging against the wall of the house included the table in a dim half circle of light. They sat there and ate. Tony had scrubbed himself for the meal. His hair was soaked in water and sleeked back over his round skull. A man in the desert might be willing to pay five dollars for as much water as went to the soaking of that hair.

Everything was good. Tony knew how to cook, and he knew how to keep the glasses filled with his wine.

"This is old wine. This is my father's wine. Eleven years old," said Tony. "You look at the light through it. You see that brown in the red? That's the soft that time puts in good wine, my father always said."

"What killed your father?" asked Durante.

Tony lifted his hand as though he were listening or as though he were pointing out a thought.

"The desert killed him. I found his mule. It was dead, too. There was a leak in the canteen. My father was only five miles away when the buzzards showed him to me."

"Five miles? Just an hour — Good Lord!" said Durante. He stared with big eyes. "Just dropped down and died?" he asked.

"No," said Tony. "When you die of thirst, you always die just one way.—First you tear off your shirt, then your undershirt. That's to be cooler.—And the sun comes and cooks your bare skin.—And then you think there is water everywhere, if you dig down far enough. You begin to dig. The dust comes up your nose. You start screaming. You break your nails in the sand. You wear the flesh off the tips of your fingers, to the bone." He took a quick swallow of wine.

"Without you seen a man die of thirst, how d'you know they start screaming?" asked Durante.

"They got a screaming look when you find them," said Tony. "Take some more wine.—The desert never can get to you here. My father showed me the way to keep the desert away from the hollow. We live pretty good here? No?"

"Yeah," said Durante, loosening his shirt collar. "Yeah, pretty good."

Afterward, he slept well in the hammock until the report of a rifle waked him and he saw the color of dawn in the sky. It was such a great, round bowl that for a moment he felt as though he were above, looking down into it.

He got up and saw Tony coming in holding a rabbit by the ears, the rifle in his other hand.

"You see?" said Tony. "Breakfast came and called on us!" He laughed.

Durante examined the rabbit with care. It was nice and fat and it had been shot through the head. Through the middle of the head. Such a shudder went down the back of Durante that he washed gingerly before breakfast; he felt that his blood was cooled for the entire day.

It was a good breakfast, too, with flapjacks and stewed rabbit with green peppers, and a quart of strong coffee. Before they had finished, the sun struck through the east window and started them sweating.

"Gimme a look at that rifle of yours, Tony, will you?" Durante asked.

"You take a look at my rifle, but don't you steal the luck that's in it," laughed Tony. He brought the fifteen-shot Winchester and handed it to Durante.

"Loaded right to the brim?" asked Durante.

"I always load it full the minute I get back home," said Tony.

"Tony, come outside with me," commanded Durante.

They went out. The sun turned Durante's sweat to hot water, and then dried his skin so that his clothes felt transparent.

"Tony, I gotter be damn mean," said Durante. "Stand right there where I can see you. Don't try to get close. . . . Now listen . . . The sheriff's gonna be along this trail some time today, looking for me. He'll load himself and all his gang up with water out of your tanks.

Then he'll follow my trail across the desert. Get me? He'll follow if he finds water on the place. But he's not gonna find water."

"What you done, poor Dick?" said Tony. "Now look. . . . I could hide you in the old wine cellar where nobody . . . "

"The sheriff's not gonna find any water," said Durante. "It's gonna be like this."

He put the rifle to his shoulder, aimed, fired. The shot struck the base of the nearest tank, ranging down through the bottom. A semicircle of darkness began to stain the soil near the edge of the iron wall.

Tony fell on his knees. "No, no, Dick! Good Dick!" he said. "Look! All the vineyard. It will die. It will turn into old, dead wood, Dick," he pleaded.

"Shut your face," said Durante. "Now I've started, I kinda like the job."

Tony fell on his face and put his hands over his ears. Durante drilled a bullet hole through each tank, one after another. Afterward, he leaned on the rifle.

"Take my canteen and go in and fill it with water out of the cooling jar," he said. "Snap into it, Tony!"

Tony got up. He raised the canteen, and looked around him, not at the tanks from which the water was pouring so that the noise of the earth drinking was audible, but at the rows of his vineyard. Then he went into the house.

Durante mounted his mule. He shifted the rifle to his left hand and drew out his heavy Colt from its holster. Tony came dragging back to him, his head down. Durante watched Tony with a careful revolver but he gave up the canteen without lifting his eyes.

"The trouble with you, Tony," said Durante, "is you're yellow. I'd of fought a tribe of wildcats with my bare hands, before I'd let 'em do what I'm doin' to you. But you sit back and take it."

Tony did not seem to hear. He stretched out his hands to the vines.

"Ah, my God," said Tony. "Will you let them all die?"

Durante shrugged his shoulders. He shook the canteen to make sure that it was full. It was so brimming that there was hardly room for the liquid to make a sloshing sound. Then he turned the mule and kicked it into a dogtrot.

Half a mile from Tony's house, he threw the empty rifle to the ground. There was no sense packing that useless weight, and Tony with his peg leg would hardly come this far.

Durante looked back a mile or so later, and saw the little image of Tony picking up the rifle from the dust, then staring earnestly after his guest. Durante remembered the neat little hole clipped through the head of the rabbit. Wherever he went, he never could return again to the vineyard in the desert. But then, commencing to picture to himself the arrival of the sweating sheriff and his posse at the house of Tony, Durante laughed heartily.

The sheriff's posse could get plenty of wine, of course, but without water a man could not hope to make the desert voyage, even with a mule or a horse to help him on the way. Durante patted the full, rounded side of his canteen. He might even now begin with the first sip, but it was a luxury to postpone pleasure until desire became greater.

He raised his eyes along the trail. Close by, it was merely dotted with occasional bones, but distance joined the dots into an unbroken chalk line which wavered with a strange leisure across the Apache Desert, pointing toward the cool blue promise of the mountains. The next morning he would be among them.

A coyote whisked out of a gully and ran like a gray puff of dust on the wind. His tongue hung out like a little red rag from the side of his mouth; and suddenly Durante was dry to the marrow. He uncorked and lifted his canteen. It had a slightly sour smell; perhaps the sacking which covered it had grown a trifle old. And then he poured a great mouthful of lukewarm liquid down his throat. He had swallowed it before his senses could give him warning.

It was wine!

He looked first of all toward the mountains. They were as calmly blue, as distant as when he had started that morning. Twenty-four hours not on water, but on wine!

"I deserve it," said Durante. "I trusted him to fill the canteen. . . . I deserve it. Curse him!" With a mighty resolution, he quieted the panic in his soul. He would not touch the stuff until noon. Then he would take one discreet sip. He would win through.

It seemed that hours went by. He looked at his watch and found it was only ten o'clock. And he had thought that it was on the verge of noon! He uncorked the wine and drank freely, and corking the canteen felt almost as though he needed a drink of water more than before. He sloshed the contents of the canteen. Already it was horribly light.

Once, he turned the mule and considered the return trip; but he could remember the head of the rabbit too clearly, drilled right through the center. The vineyard, the rows of old twisted, gnarled little trunks with the bark peeling off . . . every vine was to Tony like a human life. And Durante had condemned them all to death!

He faced the blue of the mountains again. His heart raced in his breast with terror. Perhaps it was fear and not the suction of that dry and deadly air that made his tongue cleave to the roof of his mouth.

The day grew old. Nausea began to work in his stomach, nausea alternating with sharp pains. When he looked down, he saw that there was blood on his boots. He had been spurring the mule until the red ran down from its flanks. It went with a curious stagger, like a rocking horse with a broken rocker; and Durante grew aware that he had been keeping the mule at a gallop for a long time. He pulled it to a halt. It stood with wide-braced legs. Its head was down. When he leaned from the saddle, he saw that its mouth was open.

"It's gonna die," said Durante. "It's gonna die... what a fool I been. ... "

The mule did not die until after sunset. Durante left everything except his revolver. He carried the weight of that for an hour and discarded it, in turn. His knees were growing weak. When he looked up at the stars they shone white and clear for a moment only, and then whirled into little racing circles and scrawls of red.

He lay down. He kept his eyes closed and waited for the shaking to go out of his body, but it would not stop. And every breath of darkness was like an inhalation of black dust.

He got up and went on, staggering. Sometimes he found himself running.

Before you die of thirst, you go mad. He kept remembering that. His tongue had swollen big. Before it choked him, if he lanced it with his knife the blood would help him; he would be able to swallow. Then he remembered that the taste of blood is salty.

Once, in his boyhood, he had ridden through a pass with his father and they had looked down on the sapphire of a mountain lake, a hundred thousand million tons of water as cold as snow. ...

When he looked up now, there were no stars; and this frightened him terribly. He never had seen a desert night so dark. His eyes were failing, he was being blinded. When the morning came, he would not be able to see the mountains, and he would walk around and around in a circle until he dropped and died.

No stars, no wind; the air as still as the waters of a stale pool, and he in the dregs at the bottom. . . .

He seized his shirt at the throat and tore it away so that it hung in two rags from his hips.

He could see the earth only well enough to stumble on the rocks. But there were no stars in the heavens. He was blind; he had no more hope than a rat in a well. Ah, but Italian devils know how to put poison in wine that will steal all the senses or any one of them; and Tony had chosen to blind Durante.

He heard a sound like water. It was the swishing of the soft, deep sand through which he was treading; sand so soft that a man could dig it away with his bare hands. . . .

Afterward, after many hours, out of the blind face of that sky the rain began to fall. It made first a whispering, and then a delicate murmur like voices conversing; but after that, just at the dawn, it roared like the hoofs of ten thousand charging horses. Even through that thundering confusion the big birds with naked heads and red, raw necks found their way down to one place in the Apache Desert.